MAKE US AWARE

ISBN: 1453723382
ISBN-13: 9781453723388
Library of Congress Control Number: 2010911100

MAKE US AWARE

The Writings of
The Reverend Dr. James Leslie
Chaplain, Ohio Wesleyan University, 1960–1988

TABLE OF CONTENTS

Foreword

It was just a mud hut. The dark interior was smaller, more modest, and cooler than he had imagined it might be. A neatly made-up cot sat in one corner, but the dominant piece of furniture was a large spinning wheel, and sitting on the floor next to this simple symbol of humble hard work was a skinny old man, dressed in the sparse near-rag wrappings of a peasant.

He, on the other hand, was a sophisticated Bostonian, only 14 years of age, but already quite well-versed in the ways of the world. His father was a polished, published, and well-known professor of Old Testament Studies at a major East Coast university, and he was accompanying his father on a sabbatical that already had led them to Japan, Korea, and China, and would soon take them on to Europe and the Middle East before they returned triumphantly home to Boston.

Most of his father's sabbatical tour, from 1939 to 1940, had taken them to exotic places to meet with powerful and influential people. Today's venture seemed more like an off-road rural side trip, and part of him might well have wondered what caused his father to travel so far out of his way to spend a full day with this frail, impish-looking, soft-spoken old man. Even as he knew this meeting was distinctively different, it was not until years later that Jim Leslie would smile at his youthful innocence that day and tell me, "This is my only picture of that day—a photo of the hut, but not the man. It took me many years to realize the full significance of the day I sat and listened as my father discussed matters of faith and world affairs with Mahatma Gandhi."

Looking back on the life of the Reverend Dr. James Leslie, one could easily claim that day as the hinge on the gatepost of his world view, his theology, and his passionate role as a powerful and prophetic voice for social justice, racial reconciliation, and world peace.

Throughout his life in higher education chaplaincy, Jim Leslie's personal, emotional, theological, and ethical connection with Mahatma Gandhi reverberates like the bass drum rhythm in a symphonic orchestra. It has been the pulse of his purpose in life, and it is echoed in nearly every word he has ever written or spoken, as reflected in the following samples of his life's work and word.

For more than three decades, Jim Leslie has been my professional mentor and my personal hero. It is impossible for me to read through this wonderful collection of prayers, essays, sermons, and speeches without hearing the delightful lilt of his voice, seeing the mischievous twinkle in his eye, or feeling the passionate commitment of his soul. I wish the same for you, dear reader. Take your time with these amazing entries, and be blessed with the quiet wonder of this humble, gentle giant who so profoundly shaped the vision of Ohio Wesleyan University's first three decades of full-time chaplaincy.

THE REV. JON POWERS
UNIVERSITY CHAPLAIN
OHIO WESLEYAN UNIVERSITY, 1988–present

Introduction

On June 8, 1969, Jim Leslie, the Chaplain at Ohio Wesleyan University, gave a benediction following the Commencement ceremony. It included the following:

Go. Take your protests to remedy injustice.

Go. Take your talents to a hungry world.

Go. For Christ's sake, go, and make a difference.

AMEN.

Making a difference was a theme found often in what Jim wrote, in what he said, and in what he did. It defined his role for a quarter of a century as Ohio Wesleyan's chaplain.

From 1960 to 1988, with warmth, good humor, and tenacity, Jim Leslie was an activist, championing the causes of peace in a time of war, of racial justice in a time of segregation, and of leading a moral life in a time of cultural revolt.

All the while, he celebrated God's gift of life and love, the inner goodness of us all—his flock—which included the University's students, faculty, administrators, as well as the townspeople of Delaware, Ohio, where the University is an integral part of the community.

Jim's desire for us all to make a difference is faithfully captured in his writings. He relied on a strong faith that was itself groundbreaking, shattering the worn image of the institutional church to embrace a religious mission that valued not just faith and prayer, but also speaking out, community action, intervention, and liberation. Typical was his simple act of bearing witness in the first days of my freshman year at a vigil outside a University residence hall for four brutally murdered little girls—all victims of the Ku Klux Klan bombing of the Sixteenth Street Baptist Church in Birmingham, Alabama.

At home, racial segregation was not the only moral challenge he addressed. In an era that saw the assassinations of President John F. Kennedy, Dr. Martin Luther King Jr., and Senator Robert Kennedy, there was also the poverty and rioting in urban ghettos, the plight of migrant workers, the pockets of right-wing extremism scattered across the land, and the growing plague of the drug scene. Jim had something meaningful to say about them all.

Abroad, the divisive war in Vietnam and its mounting death toll on both sides raised other questions for Jim of what was moral, as did world poverty, starvation in Biafra, apartheid in South Africa, conflict in the Middle East and the cold war crusade against communism.

At Ohio Wesleyan and other campuses, students were faced with the perpetual moral complexities of dealing with new freedoms—coping, among other things, with shifting values, social pressures, challenges to their religious faith and, for a time, the military draft.

All of this turmoil was summed up in Jim's modest, delightfully cluttered campus office, which was plastered with scores of posters, signs, and slogans ranging from "One nuclear bomb can ruin your whole day" to "If we have love in our hearts, disagreement will do us no harm. If we do not have love in our hearts, agreement will do us no good."

He took pleasure in the cycles of university life: the beginning of the academic year, the dedication of a new running track, the formation of a new group of students committed to a cause, the coming of spring, the latest parade of happy students under caps and gowns at graduation, and the perennial return of alumni to campus events.

Although he would reject the description, his impact was legendary. Privately and publicly he counseled students in matters of morals and religion. He embraced the alienated. He celebrated the rejected. He nudged the self-satisfied. He comforted the distressed. Whether dealing with students, faculty members, or University administrators, his style always left one uplifted rather than shamed.

He was among the most inclusive of people, always remembering the usually forgotten: the cooks who prepared the meal; the cleaners who swept the floors; the stage hands who arranged the set at campus events. To the one person whose name he did forget, a student to whom he lent a few dollars, he writes an endearing, apologetic poem—"I Forgot Her Name."

He gave of himself often and generously, even in mourning the death of his infant son, offering sage advice on coping with loss in "You Mean He's Still Part of Our Family?" In that moving essay, he concluded:

> For some, the death of a loved one can destroy whatever unity a family has known. For others, who will not shut themselves off from each other, the experience can strengthen their love for one another and bring them into a closer relationship with a God who makes himself known best when his children are in trouble.

With his gentle, persuasive way, by advice and example, Jim served thousands as a moral compass, bearing witness on behalf of peace and justice at home and abroad and teaching that it is better to stand up for what's right, especially when it's easier to accept the status quo. As he put it at his own retirement: "I'd rather try and fail than fail to try."

LARRY HEINZERLING
OHIO WESLEYAN UNIVERSITY CLASS OF 1967

Prologue

1972: Commencement, Ohio Wesleyan University

Lord,
We've heard enough
We've seen enough
We've said enough to know that
There are people to feed
Love to share
Wars to stop
Now, be among us as we go and do it!

Occasional Writings

Awed by God

January 1964: Chapel Sermon

I would like to talk about some odd characteristics found among some here and hopefully growing in others.

There are two kinds of odd that I mean: awed and odd, and frequently the person who is awed is thought to be odd. He is "touched," according to many, but I would suggest that he may be touched by the kind of a power that makes a difference in his life. We should be so odd!

We like to label people as odd and dismiss them for it. You know when we do it: If he doesn't get a haircut; if he is seen with the wrong people; if he doesn't date or doesn't "make out"; if he rides a bicycle on a campus of sports cars; if he dates people from the wrong sorority, or no sorority; if he is too outspoken; if he doesn't like parties, even mild parties. But he is especially odd if he's awed by God. In some circles, this is enough to shunt him off for his four years as incurably pious.

We have labeled people as odd who are on our campus or who come to our campus, and the label has been the same as making suspect whatever they have to say.

Some of our faculty are thought to be pink, and are thus written off by some townspeople and by some students. To label a person as pro-Communist or Socialist is enough to have what he says discounted.

Wasn't it interesting that when Linus Pauling was given the Nobel Peace Prize, some leading publications considered the award a diplomatic slap in the face to the United States? When J. Robert Oppenheimer was given the Fermi Award by the Atomic Energy Commission, some of the committee even refused to be present because they felt that his opposition to the production of the hydrogen bomb was un-American.

When Frank Wilkinson was on our campus speaking about his fight to abolish the House Un-American Activities Committee, his presence raised the eyebrows of some residents of the community, the local press, and some of our students.

These three people are odd because their positions are not in agreement with others. Those who have been awed by God take on qualities that are considered odd.

Is it odd to forgive?

"One of the Pharisees asked him to eat with him, and he went into the Pharisee's house, and sat at table. And behold, a woman of the city, who was a sinner, when she learned that he was sitting at table in the Pharisee's house, brought an alabaster flask of ointment, and, standing behind him at his feet, weeping, she began to wet his feet with her tears, and wiped them with the hair of her head, and kissed his feet, and anointed them with the ointment.

"Now, when the Pharisee who had invited him saw it, he said to himself, 'If this man was a prophet, he would have known who and what sort of woman this is touching him, for she is a sinner.' And Jesus, answering, said to him, 'Simon, I have something to say to you.' And he answered, 'What is it, Teacher?'

"A certain creditor had two debtors; one owed five hundred denarii, and the other fifty. When they could not pay, he forgave them both. Now which of them will love him more? Simon answered, 'The one, I suppose, to whom he forgave more.' And he said to him, 'You have judged rightly.'

"Then turning toward the woman he said to Simon, 'Do you see this woman? I entered your house, you gave me no water for my feet, but she has wet my feet with her tears and wiped them with her hair. You gave me no kiss, but from the time I came in she has not ceased to kiss my feet. You did not anoint my head with oil, but she has anointed my feet with ointment. Therefore, I tell you, her sins, which are many, are forgiven, for she loved much; but he who is forgiven little, loves little.' And he said to her, 'Your sins are forgiven.'

"Then those who were at table with him began to say among themselves, 'Who is this, who even forgives sins?' And he said to the woman, 'Your faith has saved you; go in peace.'" Luke 7:36-50

Modern penology urges that those indicted for crimes should be treated in such a way as to make it possible for them to return to life outside of the prison walls. But critics of such a philosophy say this is wrong; we should keep them behind bars.

Is it odd to love?

Mrs. Marie Frances Tippett, the widow of the policeman who tried to disarm Lee Harvey Oswald, has received some $600,000, an exciting and invigorating expression of concern for one who is very much alone.

Mrs. Oswald, the widow of the accused slayer of President Kennedy, has been sent several thousand dollars. It is understandable that people associate her husband's assumed crime with her, but perhaps her need is greater. Is not love as essential in her life as in the life of Mrs. Tippett?

Is it odd to relate to the unlovely?

It was said of Jesus, "Look at him, a glutton and a drinker, a friend of tax gatherers and sinners." Jesus spent much time with the unloved. Were he here today, he would be with the junkies, the convicts, the pimps, the owners of houses of prostitution, the hoods, and the homosexuals, because it was his nature to be drawn to those most in need.

His story of the lost sheep being important to the shepherd, though the 99 were safe in the sheepfold, speaks to this.

Is it any wonder that Jesus was rejected by the leaders of the faith of his day? He did just the opposite of what some of them had been teaching for years. Whereas they would have walked on the other side of the road to avoid an unclean person, Jesus sought him out and stayed with him. While they would never associate with tax collectors, Jesus often dined with them; visited their homes; and even had Matthew, the tax collector, as a disciple. Even the mention of the name of a prostitute was considered evil, but Jesus praised the one who anointed his feet and worked with those who were most in need.

Recently I heard of a student on this campus who was a friend of one who is a member of a minority group and a holder of unpopular ideas. The girl was told by her associates that to continue with her friendship with the person in question was to destroy herself socially. "Don't be odd," said her friends. "Don't be different."

Is it odd to look upon people as persons?

It may seem strange to you, but some of our international students, a few of the Negroes among us, three or four Jews, and a handful of Catholic students are really persons. And if you hit them, they cry; if you shun them, they are hurt; if you trip them, they fall.

The feeling of some of our campus community is that these odd people are different—they can't be individuals—they are to be lumped with their categories: their belligerence, their clannishness, and their peculiar religious beliefs.

We consider international students as not knowing any better: "If they don't want their feelings hurt, they shouldn't come here. How are we to know they need to save face? They're different. They aren't hurt by being ignored. They are only sponges, taking all that we will give them, but not doing anything in return. They are poor students and they pass only because the instructors feel sorry for them."

And the Jews here? "They are money mad. They are only interested in medicine or law because the jobs pay so well. They aren't people. They are a bunch of Zionists who belong in Israel because they have no love for this country."

The Catholics we may consider "ignorant and closed-minded and superstitious," and we forget that if they have been in a closed society, we built the walls that made it closed when we refused to view them as children of God who are trying to do his will.

Some of us think that the biggest goal in the life of the Negro is to date and ultimately marry a Caucasian. We think they are highly motivated sexually, that they are children, and that they are pushing too far and too fast to be considered equals. "Why must they push for the vote when they still have a slave mentality? Why do they ask to be treated as equals when we whites say they aren't equal?"

It has been suggested by some that there is a movement on campus to encourage interracial dating and interracial marriage among our students. I know of no such group or movement, but I do know of those who would have people treated as persons—persons who are lovely and loving and who enjoy social relationships.

No one should be pressured into dating people whom he does not choose to date, but we are called upon to support those who choose to enjoy themselves as persons with others who are persons, who may speak differently, or who come from some other land. This is not to advocate interracial dating or intermarriage, but it is to recognize its inevitability and to suggest that people need to have the freedom to associate with whom they choose even if it is offensive to us or to our parents.

Is it odd to demand an inclusive faith?

Inclusiveness, to many people, is a sign of weakness. These people would have us be bold and strong and make demands on people before we can show them friendship. Christians are guilty of this when we substitute an authoritative answer that must be accepted in its entirety for an outgoing profession of a belief in a loving God who is concerned for all. Is it odd to say, "Come unto me," rather than, "Believe or be damned"?

A most odd character in Christian history was Giovanni Bernardone, whose nickname of Francesco came to be the name he used—Francis of Assisi. A mischievous young man who enjoyed revelry and who knew wealth, Francis gave up his enjoyable life to practice poverty and be an imitator of Christ. Listen to his Canticle of the Sun:

"Most high, most great and good Lord, to thee belong praises, glory and every blessing!

"Blessed be thou, my Lord, for the gift of all thy creatures: and especially for our brother the sun, by whom the day is enlightened. He is radiant and bright, and of great splendor, bearing witness to Thee, O my God.

"Blessed be thou, my Lord, for our sister the moon, and for the stars; thou hast formed them in the heavens, fair and clear.

"Blessed be thou, my Lord, for our brother the wind, for the air, for cloud, and calm, for every kind of weather, for by them thou dost sustain all creatures.

"Blessed be thou, my Lord, for our sister water, which is very useful, humble, chaste, and precious.

"Blessed be thou, my Lord, for our brother fire, gay, noble, and beautiful, untamable and strong, by whom thou dost illume the night.

"Blessed be thou, my Lord, for our mother the earth, who sustains and nourishes us, who brings forth all kinds of fruit, herbs, and bright hued flowers.

"Blessed be thou, my Lord, for those who pardon for love of thee, who patiently bear infirmity and tribulation. Happy are those who abide in peace, for by thee, most high, they will be crowned.

"Blessed be thou, my Lord, for our sister death of the body, from whom no living man can escape. Happy are they who at the hour of death are found in obedience to thy holy will.

"Praise ye, and bless ye my Lord! Give him thanks, and serve him with great humility! Amen."

How odd can you get? And I would spell that in both ways. We should be so awed.

Whom do we seek to please?

Those who were Jesus' critics, who were like the anchor man in a tug-of-war, who fight and kick and pull back on every opportunity to grow and change?

Those who would have us throw away all that we have known, saying that nothing of the past is of any worth?

The general public?

Are our relations with the public our clue to behavior? Is our goal compatibility, a pleasing personality, savoir faire?

The time will come when we will have to say something to someone that will not be liked, to take a stand on some issue that will destroy our popular image.

I came across the following lines recently:

"He's awed by God, but God, he's odd
And how I wish that he were not
For I could be a friend to him
And judge him fairly, not by whim
Like those about me who despise
All men who differ, with slanted eyes
Or funny names, or lips, quite thick.
O God, how odd, it makes me sick
To judge a man by outward sign
Claiming that he's no friend of mine.

He's awed by God, but God, he's strange.
He seems on fire, it's such a change
'til he latched on to every cause
That made him hope for other days,
And other methods, other ways
To end the hate and live together
And all men call each other brother.
He babbles of a coming era
When men can plan and seldom fear a
Holocaust of greed so vile
That it appears as God's denial.

He's awed by God, but God, he's odd
And how I wish that he were not."

We can dare to be awed when we are awed by God.

Why Not?

June 1968: Baccalaureate Service

College days are a mixture of ecstatic moments, when everything is going well, and periods of despair, when nothing goes right, with the bulk of time being filled with hard work giving various degrees of satisfaction to both student and instructor.

There are times when the creation of a term paper brings out the best of one's ideas and leads to a feeling of real accomplishment, when one's love is returned in kind, and when the lacrosse team wins a particularly special game.

Such times are invigorating. But there are periods when the community is drawn together because one of its number has been hurt, and when it appears that almost nothing can be done about it except to come together and ask for the help of the God who at other times would have been called dead.

Such a feeling is being experienced now in our nation and in our community. We feel the same mixture of emotions that many of our students have felt during the past four years at Ohio Wesleyan. We feel the joy of accomplishment; the feeling of pride among parents and family, many of whom have made great sacrifices to let this day be possible for those who are to receive degrees today.

But this joy is tempered by the feeling of despair because of the recent events in our nation that have snuffed out the life of one who offered so much promise for our nation and its future.

There are those who in respect for the life and memory of Senator Kennedy would have us cancel the events of today, saying that this is not in keeping with the presidential proclamation designating this day as a day of national mourning.

We feel that it is most appropriate that we continue with plans for today's events, that through these acts there might result a more intense desire to serve our God, our nation, our many callings, and our world in the spirit of this young man who was slain during the week, as well as in the spirit of one who was slain on Calvary.

In yesterday's funeral service, Senator Edward Kennedy quoted his brother as saying: "Some men see things as they are and say 'why?' I dream things that never were and say, 'Why not?'"

Why not work for those programs in our land that seek to alleviate pain, heal sickness, give men pride in themselves rather than giving honor to the destruction of villages in distant lands?

Why not work for a society that will judge a person by his potential and by his being a child of God rather than by his choice of church, nationality, or the pigmentation of his skin?

Why not extend the benefits of our technical know-how to those in our land and elsewhere who have been denied them because we have not been as concerned with building as we have in destroying?

Why not love mankind and use things instead of using mankind and loving things?

If what Robert Kennedy was saying to us in life can be heard by us through this agonizing experience of his death, then his living and his dying will not have been in vain.

Help Us Change Course

June 1970: Baccalaureate Service

Well, Lord, it's all over but the shouting. We've spent hours every night—long, long hours—when we've wondered if it was worth it.

We've written and graded the papers, talked late into the night and organized and agonized and anglicized verbs and tenses and scripts and term papers and surveys, and now it's all over, except for the shouting.

But the shouting is getting louder now. It won't stop. It won't stay put in one place. When it fades off in one area, it is picked up in another. There are people taking up many issues, many causes; taking our time; taking our thoughts; taking our preconceived ideas as to what college is all about—and questioning them.

They are suggesting that we can't use our training here as if it were gained at a finishing school. They are saying that belonging means more than having clean fingernails and knowing when to use the right fork. They won't let us rest on our laurels. They won't let us sleep our comfortable sleep of the haves when the have-nots don't even own blankets.

The shouting is getting louder. It is invading our lives. We hear it from the city. We hear it from international students. We hear it from Vietnam. We hear it from the ghettos. We hear it from the aging and from the Mexican-Americans. We hear it from the good guys and from the bad guys.

And now Women's Lib is getting into the act. They won't let us be. They won't accept our double standards. They make demands and they aren't ladylike any more, and they don't care. They request to be heard. They insist on being heard. They demand to be heard. They join with others and they say no more inequities, no more sending our children to war because war is not healthy for children and other living things.

We're overpowered by the immensity of it, Lord. So much is happening at one time that we can't control it, and when we can't pull the puppet strings to make people jump, we can't maneuver, we can't function.

We feel caught. We've talked up a storm about getting along with each other. We've talked of brotherhood. We've even set aside a week a year in honor of it. We've talked about equality for a long, long time. We continue to pass our laws in favor of it.

But still we build our high fences and emblazon on them in giant old English letters "Keep Out." And now it's catching up with us and we are revealed for what we really are—selfish and proud and arrogant.

Lord, at times we are aware of what we have done or haven't done, of what we have said or haven't said, of what we have been or haven't been. Now, Lord, now give us a vision of what we can be.

Now, Lord, now help us change our course.

Now, Lord, now make us a people for whom possibility is more important than promises, awareness is more important than awards, community is more important than coercion.

And Lord, let there be peace in our land, peace in our manner, peace in our lifestyle.

These, our persistent requests, we offer in the name of Jesus, the carpenter, whose very life was a demand for peace.

What's It All About?

June 1974: Alumni Convocation

What *is* it all about? It's about people, in a certain Midwestern college, in a county seat town, coming together to renew friendships and memories, mostly pleasurable, but some sad.

It's about remembering traditions, of gathering in this place with these people, to keep in touch with each other and the world that surrounds us and sometimes engulfs us.

It's about taking time to remember who created us and to try once again to discover why.

It's about lowering our defenses for sixty minutes to confront one another and God.

It's about a world that is hurting right now more than we can comprehend. And it's about many of us who can't remedy such hurt and who are frustrated by it.

It's about people sometimes ignoring other people in faraway places with strange-sounding names.

It's about a presence, and a power, to whom we choose to go for help.

It's about time.

It's about time we woke up to what's going on about us.

It's about time that we recognized the skills we have at our fingertips, necessary for healing, for calming, for building, and for rebuilding.

It's about minds that can sort out good intentions from difficult attempts.

It's about people who want to do what is right and often end up satisfying their own appetites, and it's about guilt feelings for doing just that.

It's about humans being inhuman to each other.

It's about the same humans being dissatisfied with what has been, and trying now to make changes, to make a difference.

It's about God, trying to get through to us, and about us, being very trying, and sometimes, sometimes, catching glimpses of God in people, in actions and even in ourselves.

It's about time to begin.

The Sick, the Dead, Diseases, and Demons

October 1979: Devotions, College Commission of the United Methodist Colleges of Ohio

Matthew 10:1, 5-8a

Jesus called his twelve disciples together and gave them authority to drive out evil spirits and to heal every disease and every sickness. These twelve men were sent out by Jesus with the following instructions: "Do not go to any gentile territory or any Samaritan towns. Instead, you are to go to those lost sheep, the people of Israel. Go and preach. The kingdom of heaven is near. Heal the sick. Bring the dead back to life. Heal those who suffer from dreaded skin diseases and drive out demons."

We, too, are given our instructions: Heal the sick, bring the dead back to life. Heal those who suffer from dreaded diseases, drive out demons.

Heal the sick.

We have been commissioned to heal the sick.

There is sickness among us when we use people and love things instead of the reverse.

We are disturbed by all the Vietnamese boat people who are flooding our country and other lands. Why do they have to upset us? We have forgotten our major role in bringing on their national disorder.

There is sickness among us when we are more interested in competition than in cooperation.

There is sickness among us when Pete Rose's value as a person is determined by the amount of money he holds out for in a baseball contract.

There is sickness among us when a punk rock band unheard of last year commands $15,000 for a single performance on a campus, but we aren't sure that we can afford to pay $1,500 for the Cleveland Symphony this year.

There is sickness among us when we have pride in our huge home with ten bedrooms and a Jacuzzi and a handball court—and high picket fences with large "Keep Out" signs.

There is sickness among us when my church has four ministers and the largest budget in town and three basketball teams and four youth choirs and an organ so fine that we can't find anyone good enough to play it.

There is sickness among us when we believe that the way to peace is to spend more money than any other country in preparing for war.

There is sickness among us when the nation's highest medal is given to those persons who kill more people than anyone else and when we call that heroism.

Raise the dead.

There are those among us who say:

"I'm only twenty-five, but sometimes I feel as though I'm at the end of my productivity." Lord, bring the dead back to life.

"My children have left home or gone to college. Life has ended for me." Bring the dead back to life.

"Hardly anyone is interested in my field. Few sign up for my classes. There are almost no majors in my field. I'm worthless and outdated." Bring the dead back to life.

"When I look around me, I see a world misusing its resources arming for an inevitable war too horrible to think about." Bring the dead back to life.

When religion should be the basis for people's communicating, it too often is the cause of problems between them.

We see Ireland torn apart because of problems between Catholics and Protestants.

We see the Middle East in constant turmoil because of Jewish-Arab hatreds. Lord, bring the dead back to life.

Those who suffer from dread diseases.

There are forms of leprosy that feed on us. Those whom I used to believe to be above suspicion, I'm not sure I trust anymore—congressmen and senators, the FBI, the CIA, the Personnel Committee.

And don't lots of students cheat on exams? And don't lots of faculty members cheat on husbands or wives? Don't lots of administrators act as puppets for the president? And don't lots of presidents jump when trustees crack their whips? And aren't all trustees power hungry? And aren't most chaplains phonies and quacks really wanting to be like Leroy Jenkins and heal people on Sunday morning television programs? Lord, heal those of us who suffer from dread diseases.

Drive out the demons.

There are lots of demons surrounding me.

I'm beginning to believe that evaluation—the one that students wrote saying that I'm a great teacher and if the college were to lose me I could never be replaced.

If I am so good at what I do, perhaps I shouldn't associate with those little people who write flattering evaluations of me hoping to get better grades.

If I can befriend the committee members who are to make the decision concerning my tenure, perhaps they'll vote in my favor.

It won't do my career any good to be seen with that rabble-rousing colleague in the faculty. I'll disassociate myself from her.

I'll take positions in my community that are approved by the city fathers; in politics, by attending the right church; by joining the right groups; by being someone who floats with the current and never swims against it.

Lord, drive out the demons in us.

Lord, heal the sick among us, bring the dead among us back to life, heal those of us who suffer from dread diseases, drive out our demons. Amen.

A Morality Tale

Undated, Children's Sermon. Read Luke 10:25-37, "The Good Samaritan"

Sarah and Betty were 11-year-old girls. Sarah's father was the chief of police; Betty's father was an electrician.

One day when they were coming home from school, Sarah asked Betty to go into a store with her. She wanted to have some fun. "What kind of fun?" asked Betty. Sarah said that she was going to show Betty how to shop without any money. "You mean window shop?" asked Betty. She knew what that was. She and her mom did that a lot.

"No," said Sarah, "more fun than that. When no one is looking we'll just take a few things that we want—and no one will know about it."

"But I'll know about it," said Betty. "No, I don't want to do that. It's not right."

"Come on scaredycat, no one will catch us; it will be fun," said Sarah.

"No," said Betty. "I won't go in with you if you are going to do that."

"Oh, all right, silly," said Sarah. "I won't."

They went in and, sure enough, Betty didn't see Sarah take anything.

When they went by the checkout counter, the clerk asked to look in their bags, which they were used to having done, and she found some items from the store in Betty's bag and nothing in

Sarah's. Well, Betty knew she hadn't taken anything, and Sarah showed that she didn't have anything.

The store manager called Betty's parents and everyone was upset.

Several people had been observing the two girls. One was a policeman who knew Sarah very well. He had been in her home and her father was his boss. He had seen Sarah take the items and put them in Betty's bag, but he thought Sarah's father would be angry with him if he said anything about it. So he walked by on the other side of the cash register and said nothing.

A minister had seen this, too, and he was concerned about it, but the parents hadn't come yet and he was already late for a speaking engagement. He was going to talk about helping people who are in trouble, and he just couldn't take the time to tell what he saw.

Now there was a circus in town, and a young boy who traveled with the circus had been shopping. People called his people gypsies. He had only one set of clothing, and it always looked dirty, and he smelled as though he needed a bath. He wore a gold earring in his left ear and he spoke with a funny accent. The kids who had been to the circus were somewhat afraid of him and poked fun at him, too.

The boy walked up to the cashier and said, "This girl didn't take them. It was the other one. This girl didn't even know they were in her bag." Well, Sarah confessed after her parents came, and then people knew that Betty hadn't stolen anything.

Which of the three people—the policeman, the minister, or the gypsy boy—acted like a neighbor to Betty?

You go, then, and do the same thing.

Prayers, Praises, and Petitions

Forgive Us

June 1966: Baccalaureate Service

When we think we are big enough, old enough, strong enough, self-sufficient enough,

Forgive us, good Lord.

When we take the world for granted and assume love and affection are due us; when we think we won't be satisfied until everyone speaks well of us,

Forgive us, good Lord.

When everything is all right—just so long as we are on top, when war in Vietnam is all right, when gunmen in ambush can shoot Negroes, when military men of whatever side spend their days seeking to hurt one another, and when we are satisfied to let them be killed,

Forgive us, good Lord.

When children are neglected by parents and parents neglected by children,

Forgive us, good Lord.

Forgive us for our complacency when the rights of men are overlooked, when we emphasize only our freedoms and not our responsibilities, when we take all too lightly what our predecessors never dreamed would be possible.

Forgive us when we act without loving, serve without following the Christ, sing our songs with no joy, and act as if it made no difference to the world that one Jesus the Christ was born into it.

Amen.

Make Us Aware

September 1967: Opening Convocation

Make us aware, good God, of all kinds of people who wish us well here: our parents; our teachers; our older brothers, who hope we can benefit from their college years; our little sisters, who don't know why we aren't at home for supper anymore.

Make us aware of the world about us: of slow death by starvation in Brazil; of rats in New York tenements; of men dying for causes that they aren't too clear about; of innocent people caught up in wars that they can't control or stop; of friends denied their places because their hair kinks at different angles from our own; of lonely people on our street or our corridors; of marriages about to break up; of people who can never laugh; of the fear of another heart attack.

God, make us aware of our chance to teach better than we have ever taught before, of our chance to begin again with a new notebook.

Make us aware of what this college has meant to many who have sat in these seats, sung our songs, cheered their throats hoarse at a game, and made great decisions about great matters that have changed them and the world about them.

God, make us aware of what our talents are. Give us a way to use them for good; give us the wisdom to change views when new insights come; and don't let us judge our roommates, but understand them; or hide behind our masks of sophistication because it is the thing to do.

And let us be free, exciting and excited human beings, in love with life.

Amen.

Love and Compassion

June 1968: Commencement Invocation

Lord, look in love and compassion upon the family of Robert Kennedy and all other families torn apart by violence. When we see wrong, let us try to right it; when we see suffering, let us try to heal it; when we see war, let us try to stop it.

May this land, so marvelous in potential, so idealistic in its founding, be commissioned to heal rather than wound, to lift up rather than knock down, that love may be involved in our solutions and that justice and compassion may once again govern us.

Forgive us for our complacency when we emphasize our freedoms and not our responsibilities and when we take too lightly the dreams of our predecessors.

Give us a vision of a world made new and a passion to accomplish that undertaking, through Christ, our brother and Lord.

Amen.

A Prayer for the Community

February 1969: Merrick Lectures Convocation

L et it be us, O God. Let it be us who can hear the winds of change about us and not be afraid.

Let it be us who can come together to wonder that you can still love us, in spite of all we have done and been and after all we have not done and not been.

Let it be us who can care for one another, who can be honest with one another, who can show love to one another.

Show us a way. Give us a dream. Send us on a mission.

Show us a way to bring dignity to our community, so that our caste systems can be torn down.

Give us a dream of a loving community that is willing to take risks to bring about that dream.

Send us on a mission:

To a roommate, who fears that he isn't really man enough and must seek ways to prove it;

To a professor whose wife is ill and needs the support of his associates;

To our community school board members, who are searching for answers to daily educational problems;

To our newspaper editors, who want to print the truth but find it hard when they have critics on all sides;

To the person who wants to trust, but doesn't dare;

To those whose childhood faith is no longer enough and who find no excitement in what they hear from churchmen.

And Lord, let us be at peace within ourselves, within our land, within our world. So may it be.

Night for So Long

November 1969: Prayer at Moratorium, Gray Chapel

It's been night for so long, Lord.

All around me I see people pulling and tugging and tearing at each other.

It's a nightmare, but it doesn't stop when daylight comes.

I don't like it. I won't settle for it. I try to get away from it, turn my back on it, hide from it.

Yesterday, I turned on the tube. I would have settled for anything, even Lawrence Welk's champagne music, but the tube wouldn't let me escape.

They were showing a special on Biafra, and the little kids had swollen bellies and sunken eyes. Their flesh hugged their bony arms, and some couldn't even sit up. And they say that since they can't bring in enough food supplies by air, they will have to let a portion of the most emaciated die without even trying to save them. I want to run from it. I want to forget that I'm part of the same race that permits that to happen.

That's bad enough, Lord, but I'm not pulling the trigger, at least not directly. But it's a different story in Vietnam. My government is involved in the bombing and the defoliation—and I'm the government and I'm pulling the trigger.

Every day the reports come in. Every hour the casualties rise. And every day's toll of the dead is supposed to make me happy because fewer of our men are being killed. I'm not supposed to mind that huge numbers of the enemy are dying. Their death rate is claimed to be 10 times that of ours. And that is supposed to make me happy.

Why should I be pleased that enemies are dying? Who says that they don't hurt? Who says that they aren't human? Who says that they don't have wives and children and parents who suffer just as my family suffers when someone hurts me?

Lord, when will we wake up from our impossible dream, our dream that we can police the world? When will we waken to our folly? When will we see that our crimes are at least as bad as those in Nazi Germany? Do we think that because we bomb villages at such high levels we can't even hear or see the bombs that we aren't involved?

Does killing hygienically make death any sweeter to us or to those we kill?

Lord, who is my brother? Only those who vote the same party, who wear the same style clothing, who speak in languages common to Latin, who worship the same God?

Lord, help us. Lord, open our eyes to simple beauty all around us. Lord, don't let us hate the haters, nor kill the killers, but neither let us encourage their hatred nor permit their killing. And give us peace. Now.

Amen.

A New Academic Year

September 1971: Invocation, Opening Convocation

Some of us weren't sure that this day would ever come, Lord, and that we would finally be here. But it is true, and we are, and some of us are scared.

For some it is so new, so frightening, so terribly important that we make the right impression and get the best start because people are watching—our parents, our instructors, fellow faculty colleagues, the personnel committee, and students we want to impress.

Some of us are just where we want to be, with interesting people, with others who care, in an institution of some repute, and now all the work it took to get here—the highway department job, the paper route, the life guarding, the babysitting—seems worth it, and it is good to have a fresh start.

And now, Lord, let us begin a new academic year with integrity. Let us be aware of the length of people's concerns and not the length of their accomplishments, of relationships between people and not the exclusiveness of those relationships, and forbid us to be complacent with a society that rejects the word peace as being subversive while at the same time finds no fault with the four-letter dirty words: bomb, tank, kill, slum, dead, poor.

Let our security be in ballots rather than bullets, in love rather than lust, and let us come together—*right now.*

Amen.

Thoughts for Alumni

June 1976: Invocation for Alumni Convocation

It seems natural to be here, Lord, to be in Gray Chapel, which has meant so much to so many, and to be in prayer, once more calling on you to be among us. May this service set the tone for our being here in this chapel and on this planet.

We want to thank you, Lord:

For our experiences here and our experiences since we left these halls, for the lessons learned, the paths chosen, the decisions made;

For cherished friendships, some that have lasted for years, others newly made, even today; and for the promise of continuing opportunities to share who and what we are;

For valued instructors, faculty members, colleagues, acquaintances from many exotic and some not-so-exotic places, for counsel given and some taken;

For the hints of what we might become and for the possibilities of learning, even now—especially now.

May we not continue to be troubled by the insecurities we knew in our youth nor be overburdened by the insecurities of our advancing years, so that we may be open to the possibility of fresh commitments to your will and your way.

May we know that it is never too late to love, to accept you, to change; never too late to be supportive, to be accepting, to say I'm sorry, to grow, to mature. Lord, when we grow up, may we show it in the way we approach others, in the way we choose lifestyles, in the people we choose to be our heroes.

Now, Lord, now, move us to our proper dedication to love people and use things rather than using people and loving things.

Now, even now, Lord, teach us to cooperate rather than to compete.

Now, Lord, now, clear up the smog of our avarice that the simplicity of love and of childlikeness can come through to support, to cleanse, to renew, and to revitalize us.

Through Christ our Lord.

Amen.

The Branch Rickey Center

October 1976: Invocation at the dedication of the Branch Rickey Physical Education Center

For dreams long in their fulfillment, we thank you, Lord.

Thank you for the example, the steadfastness, the strength, the gentleness, the single-mindedness of Branch Rickey, and that such an exciting and useful way to honor this good man has been found.

Thank you for what this structure will mean to this institution, for the possibilities of learning new skills that will stretch mind and muscle and sinew, for the efforts of those who have funded this complex, for the planning committees, the architects, the builders, for those who maintain the building, and for those who will teach and learn within it.

Lord, may this be a happy place, where learning can be fun, where bodies can be streamlined and conditioned, where friendships can be made and new techniques learned.

May what we do on this campus, in this facility, through all of our actions, give you praise and make our campus and our planet a safer, healthier place on which to live.

Through Christ our Lord.

Amen.

Middle East Peacemakers

November 1977: Invocation, Faculty Meeting

Thank you, Lord, for the Sadats and the Begins among us who are willing to risk reputation and pride and position and even lives in the interest of peace.

Let us be aware of the importance of the meeting of minds, of conciliation and reconciliation, of the deemphasizing of battle scars and the healing of ancient wounds.

May this meeting bring us together, and may what we say this night be worth hearing and what we do be worth recording.

In the name of the Prince of Peace.

Amen.

The Gift of Martin Luther King Jr.

January 16, 1978: Service Honoring the Life of Martin Luther King Jr.

Thank you, Lord, for Martin Luther King Jr., who, because of his devotion to justice and dignity and a classless society earned the antagonism of those whose life systems were threatened by the changes he promoted—but whose visions of what might be earned him peace prizes and accolades and a national holiday in his honor and the unending gratitude of people throughout this land.

Thank you, Lord, for his gentleness—like that of St. Francis of Assisi; for his compassion—like that of Florence Nightingale; for his unswerving concern for justice as in Amos' statement: "Let justice roll down like a mighty stream."

Thank you, Lord, for the insights he gained from Gandhi and his non-violent stance; for his ability to listen and to learn from the little people who had been through so much for so long.

Thank you for his complete confidence and trust in Jesus Christ—who was his brother, his companion, his guide, his inspiration—his Lord.

Thank you, God, for Dr. King's fearlessness in the face of possible assassination; his obedience in doing your will, no matter what the outcome; his unswerving devotion to aid the oppressed; his recognition by nations and leaders of lands around the world, who join us now in affirming Martin King's freedom affirmation: "Free at last, free at last, thank God almighty, I'm free at last."

Free and Challenge Us

1980: Invocation, Faculty Meeting

Lord God, free us from the weighty burdens that we carry with us:

Of being more concerned with prestige than with availability.

Of being too timid to be critics of our society.

Of being more impressed with the valuation of our colleagues than with the importance of our actions.

Challenge us to take on new burdens willingly:

Of caring for those who hurt.

Of not judging others more harshly than we judge ourselves.

Of being willing to have our voices heard over the din of inequity.

May what happens here this evening be worth doing.

Iranian Hostage Crisis

October 1980: Invocation, Faculty Meeting

Lord of all hostages, be among us in our bondage, for we are held hostage:

By our need to be better than the people who live next to us.

By our view that the United States knows what is right for the world.

By the belief that democracy, capitalism, and free enterprise are all Christian.

Turn the mirrors of the planet on us that we might see ourselves as we are seen by the world, and in our hostage state may we understand the feeling of Iranians, South Africans, Namibians, South Koreans, El Salvadorans, and others in their need to be free.

Lord, free us from such bondage.

Amen.

The Beloved Community

January 1981: Invocation, Faculty Meeting

We are grateful, O God, for what appears to be a resolution of the hostage issue.

Now free us from what keeps us hostage:

Our desire for revenge;

Our ambition;

Our pride;

Our deadlines;

Our distrust of governments foreign to us;

Our concern for four American nuns killed and our lack of concern for 10,000 citizens killed in El Salvador.

Remove our chains that we might be free again, and open, and searching again.

We pray for President-elect Reagan and those charged with governing the land, that they might succeed in resolving the complex problems our nation faces. May we come together in our several communities—racially, politically, humanly—that together we might build the beloved community.

We Cannot Merely Pray

November 1982: Invocation, Faculty Meeting

[Adapted from a prayer by Jack Reimer]

> *We cannot merely pray to you, O God, to end war;*
> *For we know that you have made the world in a way*
> *That we must find our own way to peace*
> *With ourselves and with our neighbors.*

> *We cannot merely pray to you, O God, to end starvation;*
> *For you have already given us the resources*
> *With which to feed the entire world,*
> *If we can only use them wisely.*

> *We cannot merely pray to you, O God,*
> *To root out injustice;*
> *For you have already given us eyes*
> *With which to see the good in all people,*
> *If we would only use them rightly.*

> *We cannot merely pray to you, O God, to end despair;*
> *For you have already given us the power*
> *To clear away slums and to give hope,*
> *If we would only use our power justly.*

We cannot merely pray to you, O God, to end disease;
For you have already given us great minds with which
To search out cures and healing,
If we would only use them constructively.

Therefore, we pray to you instead, O God,
For strength, determination, and willpower
To do, instead of just to pray,
To become, instead of merely to wish.
Amen.

Remind Us

April 1985: Invocation, Faculty Meeting

When we complain about snow in April, remind us of the warmth of today.

When we are distressed by too much rain, remind us of the years of drought in the Sahel.

When we gripe that we don't have the latest in sports cars or designer clothing, remind us of the victims of the bombings in Iran and Iraq.

When we think that no one cares for us, remind us of who we are and whose we are and the wonder of life.

Remembering Martin Luther King, Jr.

January 1983: Invocation, Faculty Meeting

Today marks the honoring of the birth anniversary of Martin Luther King, Jr., who gave us eyes to see, even when we will not look; and ears to hear, even when we will not listen.

Listen now, to an excerpt from his *Letters from a Birmingham Jail:*

"I must make two honest confessions to you, my Christian and Jewish brothers. First, I must confess that over the past few years I have been gravely disappointed with the white moderate.

"I have almost reached the regrettable conclusion that the Negro's great stumbling block in his stride toward freedom is not the White Citizen's Councilor or the Ku Klux Klanner, but the white moderate, who is more devoted to 'order' than to justice; who prefers a negative peace, which is the absence of tension, to a positive peace, which is the presence of justice; who constantly says, "I agree with you in the goal you seek, but I cannot agree with your methods of direct action"; who paternalistically believes he can set the timetable for another man's freedom; who lives by a mythical concept of time and who constantly advises the Negro to wait for a 'more convenient season.'

"Shallow understanding from people of good will is more frustrating than absolute misunderstanding from people of ill will. Lukewarm acceptance is much more bewildering than outright rejection."

Let us pray. Thank you, God, for this good man—and, God, raise up even among us others to take his place.

Amen.

To New Students

September 1983: Invocation, Opening Convocation

God of our past, thank you for our history, for loving families who have dreamed of this very day when their daughters and sons, nieces, nephews, and grandchildren would begin such a great adventure.

We are grateful for those who have gone before us who have made this institution what it is—with its commitment to values and its pursuit of the truth that will make us free.

God of now, thank you for today.

Don't let us become complacent with what we are or what we have when others on all sides are struggling for survival.

May what we learn here help us make changes to feed the hungry—and to raise up each person in dignity.

God of our tomorrows, awaken us to the possibilities all around us:

To challenge the lethargic;

To alert a world too accustomed to violence to a better way;

To create a community where peace is our first priority.

This prayer is offered in the name of the Prince of Peace—ever Jesus Christ.

Amen.

We Are All Worthy

February 1984: Invocation and Benediction, Black Student Program

Invocation

Lord God, creator of each one of us, thank you for the lives we have been given—for the challenges to grow and to learn that face us each day, and for all the wild possibilities available to us, if we will only see them.

Teach us to learn from the new information offered by brother Hammond. Teach us to listen for times when our friends are hurting; teach us to find ways to make our community a place in which good things can happen. And may we find more pleasure in assisting to make good things happen than in getting the credit for them.

Thank you that we are together this evening, among people who care, and that we are meeting to celebrate the dignity and the worth of all people.

This we pray in the name of the great liberator, ever Jesus the Christ. Amen.

Benediction

Lord God, as the chains of slavery were broken in Abraham Lincoln's day, as the chains of the ballot box have been broken during the lifetime of some of us here gathered, so show us how to break the chains of defeatism and procrastination and self-doubt.

And now, be among us and remain with us to challenge and to comfort, to encourage and sustain, and to make us feel that as your children we are all worthy of loving and being loved. Amen.

They Added to Our Lives

February 1984: Invocation, Faculty Meeting

Two former staff members died within the past few days. They are Bob Warner, longtime fellow worker in Buildings and Grounds and former director of that office; and Monty Hoffhines, former Director of Admissions. You may also know that Joe Rushton is in the intensive care unit of Riverside Hospital with burns to his head and arms. It seems appropriate that the invocation recognize these colleagues.

Let us pray for these our brothers, and for sisters and brothers we know to be hurting.

Lord of all life, we are grateful for the lives of Bob Warner and Monty Hoffhines, who, while among us, added to our lives, strengthened our friendships, and expanded our frames of reference.

Be close to those who hurt because of Bob and Monty's deaths—and may their influence continue and the tasks left undone be undertaken by those who share their passion for them. We do not know what form of existence the future holds for any of us, but we affirm that the future is in your love and compassion.

We also pray for the recovery of Joe Rushton—that the skilled hands of lab technicians, ward clerks, candy stripers, physicians, nurses and physical therapists may bring him to restored health and that through it all may be discerned your healing power and your tender care.

And, Lord, may we not wait until people are hospitalized or seriously ill to tell them how much we care for their welfare and how much we appreciate their gifts—even as we would tell you now how much we need your power and your presence here—in this place and at this hour.

Amen.

Let Us Be Healers

June 1984: Invocation for Distinguished Achievement Citation Day, Alumni Weekend

Lord, give us eyes to see beyond our Jacuzzis and our jeans. Give us ears to hear more than the stock market reports and the neighbors who are fighting again. Give us lips to speak more than the usual comments on the weather and the bridge club.

Good God, make us aware of our world and those who hurt; those who need our skills, but can't find us; those who need our talents, but are afraid of us; those who need our compassion, but who hear only our threats.

In a world of animosity, let us be healers.

Amen.

Privileges Taken for Granted

May 1984: Invocation, Faculty Meeting

God, we are grateful that none of the students in the Women's House was injured in Sunday's fire.

We pray for other victims of fire who have no friends to room with or clothes to share.

Lord, when we complain about not having the latest in footwear, remind us:

Of those who have no feet;

Of those in countries whose economy is destroyed by inflation and who fear for the future;

Of those who are always hungry at the day's end;

Of those who must steal to live;

Of those who have no hills or vacation spots and no trips to Hawaii to remember;

God, open our eyes to the privileges we take for granted.

Amen.

When to Remind Us

September 1985: Invocation, Faculty Meeting

When we are timid about showing that we care about being hurt, about meeting people, about rejection,

When we are fearful of losing face if we take an unpopular stand,

When we are so much involved with our minor crises that we ignore Mexican earthquakes and CIA-sponsored infiltration into Nicaragua,

When we are so preoccupied with the denials of human rights in the Communist bloc that we ignore the abuses of power in our own land,

When we think we have it made because we have a retirement program, tenure, two cars, and too much to eat at dinner this evening,

Remind us of the real world, much of which is hungry now, and homeless now, and without the promise of a reasonable future.

Good God, remind us.

Amen.

A New Track

October 1985: Invocation for the dedication of a new track at Ohio Wesleyan University

ISAIAH 40:28-31

Don't you know? Haven't you heard?
The Lord is the everlasting God; creating all the world.
God never grows tired or weary.

God strengthens those who are weak and tired, even those who are young and grow weak.

Young men and women can fall exhausted. But those who trust in the Lord for help will find their strength renewed.

They will rise on wings like eagles; they will run and not get weary.

They will walk and not grow weak.

Let us pray.

Good God, open our eyes to be aware of those who can never run.

Open our ears to hear the cries of those who cannot walk.

Open our mouths to speak for those who don't have the ability, or the courage, or the capacity to defend themselves.

Let us not be satisfied with having built such a great facility as this until the athlete-scholars who use it convert the skills gained here into ways to improve health and establish trust and peace.

Amen.

Apartheid

October 1985: Apartheid Vigil

Sovereign God, when we are annoyed that we don't have change in our jeans for a Snickers bar, remind us of South African black children who have never tasted a Snickers bar and who are hungry tonight—and every night.

When we complain that there are not enough patrol cars for our campus security, remind us of the South African police who are shooting demonstrating black South Africans at this very hour.

When we take so lightly the fact that Americans are casual about voting at elections, remind us of South African blacks who have no vote and who are giving their lives to gain it.

When we take for granted our freedoms—our education, our four-bedroom houses and filled two-car garages, remind us of those who have never been free, who have had no formal education, who are crowded into makeshift shacks, and who may never have enough resources to even rent a car.

Don't let us be satisfied with this. May we not rest until justice is done and peace attained.

Amen.

Remind Us Again and Again

September 1986: Invocation, Faculty Meeting

G od of all history, keep us aware of our own history.
When we praise our land for our freedoms, remind us of slave ships and burning crosses.

When we despair over a world in revolt, remind us of 1776.

When we decry terrorism from Libya and the PLO, remind us of our warplanes over Vietnam and Laos and of our recent bombings of Libya.

When we complain about the present generation of students, remind us of what it was like to be eighteen and away from parental control.

And although we may forget our own stupidities, let us never be so callous that we forget your love for us and for being given a second and a third and a fourth chance.

Amen.

Help Us Be Grateful

November 1986: Invocation, Faculty Meeting

When we cannot decide which tour to take during the Christmas break, remind us, God, of those who have no country to leave.

When we cannot lose the pounds that we have promised ourselves we would, remind us, God, of those who cannot remember when their stomachs were full.

When we are overpowered with paying for two cars and a summer home, in addition to our home in town, remind us, God, of refugees who live in cardboard shacks.

When our children do not make the honor roll consistently, remind us, God, of children who have no schools to attend.

When we complain that we are overloaded with teaching responsibilities, too many advisees, and an unlimited stack of papers to grade, remind us, God, of those whose poor health prevents them from working at all.

Help us to be grateful for what we have and for who and whose we are.

Amen.

We'll Be Free at Last

September 1987: Invocation, Faculty Meeting

Dear parent God, who would not enslave us or have us enslave others:

Free us from out-of-synch patriotism that devalues other loyalties;

Free us from out-of-synch piety that ignores population problems, the role of women, and the possibilities of a married priesthood;

Let us not measure success by declaring as winners those who die with the most toys, the most bombs, the largest bank accounts, the most debtors;

Free us to join with the Cesar Chavezes and the Winnie and Nelson Mandelas and the Jacques Cousteaus and the Martin Luther Kings of the world and, with them, be free at last, free at last, thank God almighty, free at last.

Keep Perspective

October 1987: Invocation, Faculty Meeting

Good God, forgive us when we are so concerned for the welfare of an 18-month-old child discovered in an illegal drug-making laboratory and for the condition of Nancy Reagan, recently diagnosed with breast cancer, but so unconcerned for street people, AIDS victims, and the world's hungry.

Forgive us for our pride in the destruction of an oil terminal in the Persian Gulf, when we have exacerbated that conflict.

Forgive us for being more concerned with the fate of the stock market than we are the bulk of the world's population, which has no funds to invest.

Forgive us for demanding concessions from the Sandinistas and then changing the rules when they agree to them.

Forgive us for our national chauvinism.

Forgive our childish ways, and may our leadership on this campus and in the wider community be guided by compassion and concern for individual and national integrity.

Amen.

Let There Be More

April 1988: Benediction for the Mock Democratic Convention

L et there be more than talk.
Let there be more than easy promises.
Let there be more than clever phrases and pressured votes.
Let there be justice. Let there be peace. Let there be commitment to a world made new.
Now, go in peace, and may the peace of God go with you.
Amen.

Adieu

April 18, 1988: Final faculty meeting invocation as Chaplain at Ohio Wesleyan

Thank you, Good God, for the chance to use our talents to assist the curious and to prod the careless. Thank you for the opportunity to cooperate more than to compete and to deal more with social conscience than social ladders. Thank you for this place, these folk, and for all the wild possibilities in the future.

Amen.

May This Make a Difference in Our Lives

May 8, 1988: Final Commencement invocation as Chaplain at Ohio Wesleyan

God of all time,
   Thank you for this time.
For all that has gone before.
For the dream of what might be and now.
For family expectations, satisfaction, pride, tradition.
For what families have done, and done without.
For honor rolls and late-night term paper preparations.
For the overcoming of disappointments and the learning from critical mistakes.

God of all our possibilities,

Challenge us to see beyond the seemingly impossible problems in Northern Ireland, the Middle East, the Persian Gulf, South Africa; among the homeless, the hopeless, the jobless, the foodless, the substance abusers, to find solutions that will allow us and them to live together productively as your family.

God of all our tomorrows,

May what has happened during these years make a difference in our lives, our nation, your world.

Thank you that we are here, that finally We have arrived at this Commencement time, and most of all, for your continuing presence and your loving concern.

Amen.

Happenings

There's Something Happening Here

1969: Student Religious Happening

What on earth is this all about? One would think that when
you go to a religious service the least that you could expect
is that it would look like a church. That you would be using hym-
nals. That there would be a choir and an organist present. That
there would be flowers and a beautiful cross. Why the change?
Why not do things as we have always done them? When everything
else is changing, why do they have to change the service of worship
as well?

It has changed. The world has changed, and our understanding
of involvement has changed. Things aren't the same any more. We
don't have the same kind of security that we had when the students
were the silent generation way back in the bad old days. We can't
feel comfortable and superior any more, the way we used to when
we read of the high jinks of students swallowing gold fish or sitting
on flag poles. We don't have any more dance contests to see who
can stay on his feet the longest. Our students don't hula hoop by the
day or push peanuts with their noses by night.

It's changed. Now they challenge our right to make war, not
love; now they demand an accounting of our manufacture of hydrogen bombs and chemicals for dealing out death. Now they say
they won't fight in a war that can have no positive ending—a war
in which everyone has to lose.

Is nothing sacred anymore? Now they see that the very institution of religion that has encouraged their freedom has become despotic. Now our whole society is being challenged to change. Listen. Listen. Listen. There is a future. There is hope. There is affirmation. There is God.

(Everyman seated on a park bench on an empty stage. He should represent a person of middle age or indefinite age.)

EVERYMAN

They are all demanding that I change. They've changed my street name. They've given me a new telephone number and an area code; they've changed the size of my car tires. They seem to be trying to make a number out of me. At my bank they won't cash my check unless I have a series of undecipherable numbers on it. They won't even let me use counter checks anymore. I must have my own checkbook, and I can never remember to bring it with me.

Everything is different now. They don't want to deliver my mail unless it has a zip code on it. I can't even give blood unless I can tell them what my blood type is. And they do all this so that I will feel more secure. But I've got news for them. I don't feel secure. Not at all.

I'm on edge most of the time. The very things that were certain and permanent, the things that held my world together, are changing so fast that they are no longer foundations for my life.

I am told that I can't respect law officers anymore. I hear that the universities that have been the champions of the open mind are now being challenged to defend themselves.

When I was a boy, I looked up to older people with respect. I would always answer 'Yes, sir,' when I was spoken to. Nowadays, the young people are not only disrespectful, they ignore me altogether. I can't stand that.

I don't enjoy living in today's world. It is too fast. There is nothing sacred anymore. God is dead. Patriotism is dead. Morality is dead. But I'm not ready to die. I've worked too long and too hard for what I have, for what I am. I want to enjoy all of this, now that I have earned it. But I'm finding it hard to see what is enjoyable anymore.

(Commotion at end of stage. Several people carrying picket signs are in an argument about something.)

EVERYMAN

"That's what I mean. It's people like that who give me cause for unrest. They are challenging almost everything I believe in. I don't like it. I don't like them. They are threatening my peace."

(People with picket signs come to center stage.)

[If Guns are Outlawed Only Outlaws Will Have Guns
America: Love it or Leave it
Keep the U.S. out of the U.N. and the U.N. out of the U.S.
Peace
Bring the Boys Home Now
Get Out of Vietnam]

CONSERVATIVE

Why don't you take a bath? Why don't you cut your hair? Why don't you act your age? Why don't you leave the running of the war to the generals?

LIBERAL

I took a bath once. What good did it do me? I like my hair this length. I am acting my age. For once in my life I'm acting responsibly. Since when do a general's stars mean he knows anything about people, and starvation, and pain?

CONSERVATIVE

You young punks are destroying our world. You and your ideas for change. You will ruin everything!

LIBERAL

We're trying to save the world, and it's got to change to be saved. Sounds like a sermon, doesn't it?

CONSERVATIVE

What do you know about sermons? When was the last time you were in a church?

LIBERAL

What do you know about Christianity? When was the last time you put your high-sounding phrases into use?

CONSERVATIVE

I have gone to church every Sunday of my life. A perfect record.

LIBERAL

Has it made even a bit of difference to society? If not, how perfectly awful!

CONSERVATIVE

At least it keeps me away from punks like you!

LIBERAL

That's the trouble with your kind of Christianity. It's found only in the church. It doesn't speak to the world.

CONSERVATIVE

But the world is no good. We've got to save it by showing it the right way. We've got to keep it from changing.

LIBERAL

You're wrong. You're dead wrong. The world is in trouble. We've got to love it by working within it and changing it into a better place.

CONSERVATIVE

Why do you want to change it?

LIBERAL

Why are you so uptight about change?

(Young person comes out on stage—approaches Everyman. He's playing a guitar, quietly, and singing to himself.)

EVERYMAN

I like your music. What is it?

GUITARIST

Oh, something that's being sung these days.

EVERYMAN

I can't put my finger on it, but there's something different about your music. It's not like the music of my day.

GUITARIST

What do you mean?

EVERYMAN

It's hard to explain. I don't know if it is the beat or the harmony or the loudness of the sound or the intensity of your music. Do you see what I mean?

GUITARIST

I think the difference is in the words. We sing message songs now. The words and music may not be better or worse than they were in your day, but the emphasis is different. Our songs often tell a story, or put across a message.

EVERYMAN

In my day things seemed so much simpler. I guess I liked them that way. We thought we knew right from wrong. All we needed to do was set it to rhyme. But things aren't as simple as we used to think they were. They've changed.

GUITARIST

They probably never were simple. We are the simple ones when we take serious matters too lightly.
(Sing: "Reach out of the Darkness," and "The Song is Love")

GUITARIST

There is another song that most everyone here would know. Join in singing "Born Free," won't you? *(Sing with audience)*

(Long-haired, casually dressed person comes on stage, carrying anti-war symbols. Sets up table for draft counseling.)

AUDIENCE MEMBER #1

You draft dodger. My brother is in Vietnam right now, fighting for his country so you can be here at school, knocking the military and living your comfortable life. If I had my way, the law would take care of you good and proper—have you in jail until you see the light.

AUDIENCE MEMBER #2

If you are talking about patriotism, he's much more of a patriot than you are. He's trying to defend his country, and dignity, and humanity, not just here but in Vietnam and all over.

AUDIENCE MEMBER #3 (CRITIC)

How dare you call him a patriot? He probably burns the flag of his country. He probably burns draft cards, or encourages others to do it.

AUDIENCE MEMBER #4 (CONSCIENTIOUS OBJECTOR)

When my country does some of the stupid things it has done, then I do it no service to say nothing. I love my country. I love it so much I must change its direction.

CRITIC

What good do you think you can do—you, a single person up against the military in this country?

CONSCIENTIOUS OBJECTOR

You've made my point. It's because the system is so big and is doing so much to control us that I'm trying to change it.

CRITIC

Do you think you can do any good? Do you think that your protests can change it?

CONSCIENTIOUS OBJECTOR

If I don't do something, I'm afraid no one else will either. I can't sit back and let this murder go on.

CRITIC

Are you calling my country a murderer?

CONSCIENTIOUS OBJECTOR

I'd rather not, but if the shoe fits, what the difference between the gas chambers in Germany and the bombing of villages in Vietnam? The end result is the death of innocent people.

CRITIC

But you are just looking at one side of it. We're caught in a struggle between good and evil.

CONSCIENTIOUS OBJECTOR

And which side are we on? I'd like to change that. I'd like us to be as good as we claim.

CRITIC

You're still a coward. Anyone who won't defend his country doesn't deserve the protection of the law.

AUDIENCE MEMBER #2

But he's defending his country, and he is a citizen and deserves the same protection as any other citizen.

EVERYMAN

I don't understand it. It used to be so simple. My country was what I could believe in. Everyone respected the flag. No one ever thought of picketing the president or pouring paint over his car, or lying on the street in front of it. It's changing too fast for me.

(Reading about change)

(Prayer)

Let's Celebrate Some Things

August 1985:A Student-led Sunday service for New Student Orientation
Begin with guitar music from Cabaret

READER 1

Welcome to college days. Welcome. Welcome new knowledge days. Welcome. We will be speaking of God's gift so great. A new beginning of college years so have no fears, and welcome to things so new. Welcome. Expand your mind, explore new fields. Take a good look.

READER 2

Do you know why I call this a celebration? It's because I celebrate balloons, parades and chocolate chip cookies. I celebrate seashells and elephants and lions that roar.

I celebrate seeing: bright colors, wheat in a field, tiny wild flowers.

I celebrate hearing: waves pounding, the rain's rhythm, soft voice.

I celebrate touching: toes in the sand, a kitten's fur, another person.

I celebrate the sun that shines slap-dab in our faces.

And I celebrate the greening of the world, the life-giving green, the hope-giving green.

I celebrate anger at injustice.

I celebrate tears for the mistreated, the hurt, and the lonely.

I celebrate the community that cares. I celebrate the time when we made it, when we answered a cry, when we held to our warm and well-fed bodies a cold and lonely world.

I celebrate the times when we let God get through to our hiding places, through our maze of meetings, our pleasant façade, deep down to our selfhood, down to where we really are.

Call it heart, soul, naked self; it's where we hide.

Deep down away from God and away from each other.

It's not hard to see the reasons for crying in a world where our hatred for each other is so obvious. So celebrate!

Bring your balloons and your butterflies, your bouquet of flowers.

Sing your songs, whistle, laugh; life is a celebration, an affirmation of God's love.

Surely, we should celebrate!

READER 1

We want to set the tone for our Sunday Celebration through the use of boxes. They explain what we are about—and here they are.

(Other students display NEAT RIOT)

READER 1

That can't be right. Try again
(Students change letters to ATE ONION).

READER 1

Hey, you did better than this in our rehearsal. Please, one more time.

(TOOT IN RAIN)

READER 1

Do you realize how embarrassing this is for me? You make me look foolish. Get it right this time.

(ORIENTATION)

Now, wasn't that worth waiting for?

Song: *Fiddler*

READER 1

So finally it came, what I've been waiting for.

Through grammar school and high, they've told me what's in store.

I'm sensitive right now, reacting to my peers.

Don't spindle, bend or fold, speak gently in my ears.

That's what we're here for, ORIENTATION.

Strangest of sensations, looking all around.

I meet new faces, can't remember faces, names or dates or places I've found. It must be that the word *orientation* that confuses us, which is about the only explanation I can give for the spelling errors of my efficient helpers. I would hate to have you parents and friends of our students go away thinking that this is the standard of education at Ohio Wesleyan! ORIENTATION has to do with the East—the Orient. If we face east we know where the other points of the compass are in relation to that. We have a point of reference. We know where we are; we can get our bearings and can know more about where we want to go.

READER 2

You're getting to sound like a Scout leader.

READER 1

I do, don't I? But then, I've always wanted to be a leader, to help people with directions.

READER 2

But this direction business, doesn't it sound like having to take directions from someone, like you, for instance?

Personal Writings

You Mean That He Is Still Part of Our Family?

Concerning the sudden death of Peter Leslie, 18-month-old son of Betty and Jim Leslie, in 1960

He was only 18 months old, too young to speak more than a few garbled words, too young to know fear, even fear of the panel truck that was to hit him; too young to be very steady on his chubby legs, but not too young to walk into the path of the vehicle; not too young to die.

"Why did Peter die, Mommy?"

"Why did that nasty old truck have to hit him?"

"Is he cold under the ground?"

"Can he breathe?"

"Did they put him in the coffin in his new play suit?"

"If he wakes up, what will he do?"

The questions kept coming. The questions that hurt, that couldn't be answered adequately, but that couldn't go unanswered. They were not couched in soothing words. They reflected the sudden loss of a brother, long hoped for and greatly loved. There is no such idea as tact for a child, especially a child who wants satisfactory answers to questions that have been asked for centuries with the same inadequate replies.

The curious, alert minds of Peter's sisters could not grasp what had happened. The girls knew he was gone, that neighbors had repainted his room and boxed up his toys and clothes for the hard decisions of another day. They knew that all the food and cards and phone calls had something to do with the desperate way people wanted to help, to show their love, and to keep themselves from thinking about how they would have felt had their sons been the victims of such an accident.

How can a family face up to death and not be destroyed by it? The parents were tempted to retreat to their rooms, to their tears, to the isolation of their grief. They would have liked to have made no decisions, handled no daily problems, avoided household routines, but the overpowering insistence of their children's needs would not let them. There were beds to make, noses to wipe, shoes to lace, fights to arbitrate, TV antennas to adjust, stories to read, shoulders to cry upon, children who needed piggy back rides, and backs whose burdens were eased with the weight of children.

There were those who would have had the children silenced lest their persistent questions and comments bring back a flood of tears and memories. But the parents could not have it so. Peter had been and would continue to be a part of the family unit. One could not cease to love because the recipient of that love was dead. The children and the parents could not erase even 18 months of living because it hurt to remember.

The children were part of the family, not only in happy times, but in hard times, too. Their comments were important, even necessary. In their innocence, they forced parents and friends to face up to the necessity of living in a world of extreme pain and excessive joy, of sudden death and instant happiness. The parents made no attempt to hide their tears, from each other or from their children. They tried, in their halting way, to indicate that their love for Peter was special, as their love for each child was special, and that the tears would have been the same for any of those whom they loved. Death had come. The family would not be insulated from it. Death was not the end of life, but a part of it. It was the opposite of birth, and something that was to happen to every person. In Peter's case, it happened long before it was expected. No one was ready to accept it.

The most normal reaction was to find release in prayer. It was addressed to a God who grieved with the family, whose will was interpreted not as causing the death of a baby, but as willing the solace and strength that could be found by the family as it called upon God. Each day as prayer was offered to God, Peter was included. At bedtime, as each member of the family was prayed for by name, the children would say, "and God bless our little angel Peter, who is with thee." To the more sophisticated among us the concept of angel may not be acceptable, but to the sisters and parents of that particular boy, the nature of the child most closely resembled the characteristics attributed to angels.

It took a long time, but gradually Peter could be spoken of as he had been loved. His last-acquired skill of mounting the kitchen stove by pulling out the oven racks as steps to his newfound ladder was spoken of as the children wondered what mischief he would be into in heaven. One daughter even ventured the thought that he would be having a gay time chasing lambs in his new home and, upon catching them, burying his thick little hands in their curly wool. Subsequently, when a favorite uncle died, the family spoke of his being greeted in heaven by a tiny little guide who "knew the ropes" and who would see that he was properly introduced to his new community.

Having remembered the times of special meaning with their brother and son, the family was able more and more to speak of others who had died and to remember the times that were of special meaning for them: Uncle Bill's fish face, Grammie's willingness to take out her teeth to amuse the playmates of the children, Charlie's special jokes, and Uncle Robert's carving of the turkey on Thanksgiving had new meaning for those who had enjoyed particular characteristics of friends and family during their lifetime and now were freed to enjoy them after their death.

The family circle expanded to include others who had died and were known to the family. There was sensitivity to those who were going through dark days, especially as those days were connected with death. Those who grieved for their own loss found particular support from this family, which knew what grief was. A peculiar affinity seems to be established among suffering people. Through the death experience, the family was able to include in its prayers and in its concern those who were made homeless and childless in earthquakes in Japan, landslides in Europe, bus accidents in their country. The world came to be a place where there was tragedy and injury but where there also were people who were prompted by such tragedy to fill their homes, their prayers and their benevolences with demonstrations of love for those going through grief experiences.

While the grieving family may withdraw from the community, the community may isolate itself from the family as well. Well-meaning friends, in their desire to help, may not wish to intrude upon another's grief and frequently will not call on the family. Some feel themselves to be too inadequate to express themselves and think that profound words of sympathy must be offered. It has been the experience of those who have met death that love for one's neighbor is always communicable. The presence of one's friends with or without spoken assurances of love is beneficial. It is better to err on the side of responding inadequately to a felt need than not to respond at all. Whereas Peter's family could not share the views of those who stated, "It is part of God's plan," or "He will never have any pain or have to pay taxes or go to war," or "God wanted another angel with him," it could accept the love and concern of the people who wrote or spoke in such a fashion. The words spoken were not nearly as helpful as the fact that people cared enough to speak them.

It is only natural that people should feel helpless at the time of death. Expressions such as, "If only we could do something," "Be sure to call on us if we can help in any way," are common. What can members of a family do to help another family? Here are a few suggestions:

One customary and helpful thing to do is to plan, prepare, and clean up after meals and do household chores. In one instance, families and friends were organized by a family for meals, house-cleaning, and child care for a full week. Placemats, centerpieces, decorated napkins, and flower arrangements were prepared by children. The women organized the house, answered phone calls, and made minor decisions about appliances and housecleaning. The men redecorated the dead child's bedroom and painted his crib in preparation for another child, soon to be born.

At the time of death and shortly afterwards, the grieving family is deluged with flowers, cards, phone calls, visitors, and family. Shortly after the funeral service, life is supposed to return to normal. It is at just such a time that the concerned family can be of great help. The despair of the lonely months that follow death can be relieved by the continual attention of those who give themselves to the care of friends.

Grief knows no geographic locale. When a child is killed in one community, those who hear about it in another respond, especially if they have known such grief. Letters from concerned family (children as well as adults) help. Letters testifying to the love of God, who cares, especially at such a time, prove to be most valuable.

The family members going through a grief experience need to be together for much of it. To isolate them, by constantly taking the children away from the home, removes the possibility of children being a part of the therapeutic aspects of grief. Having the children in the home brings the family to the realization of the continuity of responsibility and the continuity of life. Therefore, this writer would caution families against trying to see that children and their parents are kept away from each other and away from the home. This is not to say that it wouldn't be valuable for members of the family to have their own interests and friends, nor should they have to remain in the home at all times; it is to suggest, however, that much can be gained by a family working through its grief as a family.

A family that understands grief can offer itself to their church to be of service at the time of death. The pastor's effectiveness may be increased many times by having parishioners who are able to minister in the name of the church.

Families can anticipate death by helping children and adults to understand aspects of it before it happens. Curious minds are interested in cemeteries, funeral processions, funeral homes, caskets. Without being lurid, families can discuss the worship of God in a funeral service, ways in which we honor people, reasons for funeral practices, and can assist the minister by letting him know that they intend a funeral service to be for the worship of God.

For some, the death of a loved one can destroy whatever unity a family has known. For others, who will not shut themselves off from each other, the experience can strengthen their love for one another and bring them into a closer relationship with a God who makes himself known best when his children are in trouble.

A Trip to Bobo-Dioulasso

Undated 1968 manuscript

The image that one has of Africa is often very misleading. When I knew it would be possible for me to lead a group of eleven students to French-speaking Upper Volta [now Burkina Faso] under the auspices of a program known as Operation Crossroads Africa, I assumed that it would be very difficult to handle the language, the heat, sanitation problems, and all kinds of unknown difficulties that I thought would surely face me. Happily, my fears were not well founded, for the heat in Delaware appears to have been much more oppressive than the dry 110 degrees in Bobo-Dioulasso, the second largest city in Upper Volta, numbering 60,000.

Operation Crossroads Africa is a voluntary work camp program that began in 1958 under the leadership of James Robinson, a Presbyterian minister from New York City. He was concerned that Americans have the opportunity to come to know the fascinating continent of Africa. It is this program that served as a model for the Peace Corps that was to begin in 1960.

We found close ties with the Peace Corps when my group (which was one of 20 groups this summer) went to Upper Volta. (Yes, look at your map. I had to do the same thing when I first heard the name of that country. It is just north of Ghana and Ivory Coast in West Africa.) It was only after Crossroads Africa had been in Upper Volta for two years that the government of that country invited the Peace Corps to come in. The main difference between the two programs is that Crossroads is for one summer, while the Peace Corps is for two years. Each Crossroads group has the support of approximately 15 student counterparts, while the Peace Corps people must make their contacts themselves.

When the driver did show up with a truck that would hold seventeen people, he put in twenty-six. Under normal circumstances this might not be too bad except that the trip (from Accra, Ghana) took nine hours and the insulation had come off the door frame, meaning that the rain of that rainy season came in by the bucketful throughout the trip. West Africa wins again! If one doesn't have a sense of humor, one can be destroyed! (Guess who the main recipient of all that water was?)

The next day proved to be interesting, with a twelve-hour trip taking us the rest of the length of the country to the border of Upper Volta. We arrived too late to find our accommodations and so spent the night on the cement floor of the frontier police station. Incidentally, cement is no more uncomfortable in Africa than it is in the United States! Our ride into Upper Volta was exciting, if nothing else, for the forty-five miles of paved roads of that country are all within the cities, so the hundred-mile trip took eight hours and many stops for the driver to keep the radiator filled with water.

Although we were going through some of the wild animal areas, where elephants, hippos, rhinoceros, crocodiles, panthers, and leopards were to be found, we only saw two monkeys! We arrived in Ouagadougou, the capital of the country, on the Fourth of July, and were very pleased to find out that the American ambassador, a former Crossroads leader, had an annual Fourth of July picnic for Americans in the community, so, between the picnic and his swimming pool, we were able to make amends for our rather hectic three-day jaunt from Accra.

Bobo-Dioulasso was the scene of our next work camp. We arrived there on July 11 and spent the next six weeks living with a group of students from that community. Along with them, we built a study hall for students who live at home and commute to school, but who do not have electricity or adequate lighting in their homes to study. Thus, they have been spending their study time under street lights in the middle of the city. With the money from a Negro junior high school in Philadelphia, we were able to build a forty-five-foot-long, sixteen-foot-wide cement block building that will be used as a community study center.

We lived in a lycée, which is a secondary school structure on the outskirts of town, and traveled to the work site each day in a rather broken-down bus that held up valiantly until the day before we left, when it sputtered its last and resigned from service.

The Africans were amazed and amused to see the North Americans working with their hands. Later, during the course of the summer, when an American came to visit us, but did not know where we lived, he asked where the Americans were and the taxi driver said, "Oh, you mean the whites who work with their hands and who have a black American with them," and took him right to where we were.

We became very well-known in the community, in part because the Africans were not used to seeing Europeans, as we were called, have their women work as well. When I say work, I mean mixing cement, carrying blocks, and digging trenches, for this was the bulk of our program there.

We found that the Africans were not all in agreement with what we were doing, for many of those who were educated felt that their education was to remove them from the necessity of manual labor. While many of them were very friendly with us and would come to the work site, they often would not work and even made comments about some of their friends who did. Although this was disturbing, it was also very interesting to see how people feel about manual labor.

We lived in a dormitory and ate in the dining room with the same students, so that by the time the six weeks were over we had a very good understanding of how these people lived and felt and what their hopes for their country's future were. Their hopes must be tempered by the fact that this is the second-poorest country in the world with an average income of $45 per person per year. The poverty of the people was easily seen when we noticed a scramble to get the empty paper bags that the cement had come in after each batch of cement was made. We were also told by some of the students that they could eat on two dollars a month while they were in school.

We found the people to be most cordial, very friendly, and very open. In walking down the street toward the work site, I would be interrupted many times by children coming out to shake hands or by others who would suddenly appear at my side and want to hold my hand and walk with me. Almost everyone would speak to us or would always respond if we spoke to them. They would ask how our families were, how our health was, or what our plans for the day were. All of this went on in French, which was quite a challenge for those of us who don't normally speak French every day, but after talking in that language for six weeks, it gave one a feeling of being able to communicate under somewhat adverse conditions.

The Africans could not understand why we have the problems that we have, why we are in Vietnam, why we have racial difficulties, and why we have as much wealth as we do. They often said, "Do you really hate the blacks in America?" These were questions that were not easy for them to ask or for us to answer. We tried to be as frank and as open as we could.

During our stay there we had a chance to visit the tiny villages, a number of other communities, and to spend considerable time in the city of Bobo-Dioulasso itself.

"Bobo" used to be the crossroads of traders coming from North African areas, so the style of buildings often reflects that area. Since the French had been in control for quite awhile, the language is French, as are many of the customs (including the delightful French bread that we had three times a day).

On August 18, we left Bobo, being seen off by twenty-eight of the friends that we had made in that city, and took the little green one-track train down into Ivory Coast, where we spent a most enjoyable eleven days in the cities of Bouake and Abidjan. Here we had a chance to see another side of Africa, for Ivory Coast is one of the wealthiest countries in Africa.

The total experience was a very positive one for me. It has given me a greater appreciation for this country, for its strengths and its weaknesses, and for what we in the Western world can offer in sympathy and in assistance to those nations that are underdeveloped and are struggling to become a part of the modern world.

The Free University

September 1970

The Free University began at Ohio Wesleyan at a time of increasing student interest in a variety of subjects not normally dealt with in their regular course work. Along with the growing activism of students came a realization that in order to be involved, one had to know more about the reasons for unrest in the nation and world, more about the background of major world problems, and more about their own views on why they are here and what they want to do about it.

The Free University has been a valuable and appropriate learning experience for us, as it provides opportunities for people to organize around a topic and deal with it as long as it interests them, without a commitment of their time beyond that interest.

It means that students can come and go around an issue, having their loyalty to the search for truth rather than loyalty toward a given organization or a meeting time or place. Thus, a student who has expertise in a particular area can announce to the campus that he is willing to share his resources with them, while knowing that he may have no response to his own enthusiasm.

This makes it possible for people on the campus who have some free time and would like to explore a number of areas other than those currently offered through the curriculum to be a part of a community of concern for that particular topic.

When we first began the Free University, there was some criticism among some faculty members that this would detract from their courses or would encourage people to think that whatever little knowledge they had was comparable to the training of the person who had secured his Ph.D. in that field. This was not borne out in the thinking of the students or in the approach to learning that has been found in our courses. Most students have not equated the Free University courses with those being taken for university credit.

On the other hand, some of the material in the Free University has been so exciting that it has redirected students in the determination of their major fields, has changed vocational interests, and has caught the imagination of some students who thought that learning was by definition a bore. The Free University has helped some to see that their ideas, skills, and interests are shared by others and that learning is exciting and makes a difference. It has provided a whole new lifestyle for some who up until now have felt that learning was just for academic credit or for a university degree.

Now, because of the Free University concept, such people realize that much of what takes place at the university outside the classroom can be very important for learning. For some, the Free University means that people heretofore overlooked have ideas worth listening to.

For others, it means that time formerly wasted in doing unimportant things can be put to good use dealing with important issues. For still others, it means that the excitement of the world of ideas has finally caught up with them. When such ideas eventuate in a commitment to bring about necessary changes in oneself or one's society, it is especially gratifying. Some courses that began in jest have ended in a serious encounter with a variety of issues that prove to be worth the time and interest of those involved.

On our campus, the Free University idea began with a group of students, faculty members, and administrators who were anxious to open up new approaches to learning. After numerous meetings were held, four courses emerged.

During its second year, the Free University was run entirely on student initiative. The fact that there has been little faculty and administrative pushing and no roadblocks thrown up has meant a great deal to the program, for, at a time of some student distrust of administration and faculty, a completely student-run program is well received. Among the courses offered on our campus have been:

- Folklore in America: Discussions, music and lectures.
- Toxic Substances: Led by a faculty member, discussing the effects and sources of poisonous substances in the world about us.
- Radical Studies: Led by two students who were working to reveal the inadequacies of our society.
- Women's Liberation: Led by students who explored the position of women in our society in an attempt to redefine femininity in honest terms.
- Pollution: Dealt with the garbage that is threatening to get our society. The garbage was not confined to sewers, but to positions of power as well.
- Witchcraft: Dealing with the Sharon Tate murders, astrology, sorcery, voodoo, and superstitions.
- Religion: A discussion centering on Far Eastern religions, but its direction was always left up to the individuals most concerned with the course.
- Anarchy and Education: An attempt to explain the modes of anarchy and current experimental approaches to education.
- Non-English and Modern American Poetry: A study of essential but neglected poets of the United States and Europe.
- Population: A program led by professors of economics and zoology and a pre-med senior student. This course deals with birth control, death control, legal difficulties, and the like.
- Hare Krishna: The International Society for Krishna-Consciousness presents the ecstatic state of Krishna-

Consciousness by awaking the minds of people everywhere to their original eternal absolute nature. This course was led by the Krishna Society in Columbus.

- Birth Control: Directed by the Planned Parenthood Association of Columbus. The content of the course was determined by the students, usually centering on concerns that are raised in its initial sessions.
- A Course in Current Events: An unstructured course dealing with the interests of the students at that particular time.
- A Course in Welfare: Led by a former director of the Franklin County Welfare Department, a state representative on the Ohio Commission for Updating Welfare, and students who have been involved in various welfare systems throughout the country.

The welfare course is likely to be incorporated into the regular university curriculum because of the number of people interested in it, the able resources that have been used, and the national interest in welfare rights. It may be that other courses will become a part of the regular curriculum, although the proponents of the Free University feel that there is as much, if not more, to be gained by keeping it outside of the formal academic structure, so that the course content will not need to be approved by any faculty committee or department. If interest were to lessen in the issue, the students would not be required to maintain their attendance and support of a given course.

The threat to individual faculty members seems to come from the lack of stimulation found in some of their courses as well as from the embarrassing questions asked by inquisitive students who are willing to challenge inaccuracies and ineptness on the part of their instructors. Within the Free University scheme, with no credit being offered, the instructors, be they students or faculty, are not as likely to feel threatened by those who might know more than they. As a matter of fact, such people are welcomed and encouraged to be involved as they help share their knowledge about a given subject.

As would be expected, some of the courses in the Free University are primarily lecture-type courses and some turn out to be sharing courses. The sharing-type courses are those in which students may have had more exposure than a given instructor (folk music, radical study, unstructured courses, and the like).

In addition to the Free University, and almost identical to it, has been a coalition of a number of student bodies on many Ohio campuses. The Coalition at Ohio Wesleyan began at the time of the Kent State University deaths and the entry of American troops into Cambodia in the spring of 1970. Students organized into committee structures to educate themselves and the community as to the issues at hand. Among the committees are Community Action Group, Political Action Committee, Draft Committee, Welfare Rights Committee, Economic Boycott Committee, Fairness Committee, and Research and Education Committee. The spontaneity of the Coalition and its ability and willingness to tackle seemingly impossible odds illustrates the seriousness as well as the optimism of the current student mind. It is an exciting time to work in the university!

Moratorium on Vietnam

October, 1970: Ohio Wesleyan Moratorium on Vietnam

The committee had planned on a maximum of 200 people. They wanted to begin the observation of the October 15 Moratorium on Vietnam with a memorial service for those who had died in the Vietnam war, but more specifically for the Ohio Wesleyan students who had been killed in it.

By 11:45 p.m. on October 14, Phillips Auditorium was already filled. It seats 250. It was too cold to hold the meeting outside, so attempts were made to open Gray Chapel for the midnight program. By midnight some 900 people had arrived, using all available doors to gain entrance.

"Who can handle the lighting?"

"What about mikes?"

"No, we can't use the stage. Those sets are for the play tomorrow night."

"Hey, the student handling lights for the play says he'll stay and work the spots."

"The mikes are locked up some place; you'll just have to speak up."

Confusing? That's the understatement of the day, but that is also the condition of the times. What could have been a chaotic event of some proportion turned out to be a confrontation of people and views of some significance.

Five Weathermen (the radical arm of the Students for a Democratic Society) who were visiting Delaware were introduced and began making their pitch for financial help for some of their number who were involved with court and lawyers' fees, having run afoul of the law in their support of protestors at the Democratic Convention in Chicago in 1968. The Weathermen urged students to join their cause and to give what they could by putting money in the motorcycle helmets and boxes being passed around.

A lively discussion followed. People were speaking to each other and to the issues. Soon, a female student, tears streaming down her face, called for people to reject the approach of the Weathermen, saying that the Moratorium was a call for the cessation of violence in Vietnam and everywhere, and what was asked for by the Weathermen was a continuing of confrontation and violence. First the students applauded, then they cheered, then they stood and agreed with voices and whistles.

The dialogue continued between those who wanted the Moratorium to be a sign of a call to revolt and those who saw it as a witness for peace. The former were few in number but most vocal. The latter were the vast majority who let it be known that they were searching for peace. Large numbers concluded the service with a candlelight procession across the campus, while many remained to debate the issues raised.

On October 15, a crowded Welch dining room was the scene of morning presentations by faculty and students raising historical, ethical, and economic questions having to do with the Vietnam War. An outdoor Chapel Happening at Phillips Hall brought together several hundred students and faculty to listen to and participate in songs, prayers, and pleas for peace. Discussion, singing, debates (large and small on issues big and little) continued as knots of people met all over the campus to deal with the war that nobody wants.

The faculty already had held a special meeting to determine its role in the Moratorium, concluding that faculty and students should use the freedoms already given them to use material in the classroom that would be relevant to the issues or to combine, dismiss, or cut classes in favor of special events that were being held. Many classes brought into their discussion the poetry of war, the history of Vietnam and the present conflict, the ethical demands placed upon the nation and the individual soldier, and the like.

Lectures and debates filled the afternoon and evening, rounding out a day of concerned activity, study, and joining with other communities across the nation in what must have been the most concentrated plea and demonstration for peace in our nation's history. The Moratorium on Ohio Wesleyan's campus offered proof that our students are concerned for a peaceful solution to world problems, that they are not examples of the domino theory of espousing whatever is offered to them, and that rational people may disagree yet may remain in contact with each other.

A View of Christian America

Undated

Abdul had lived all of his years in a tiny sheikdom in the Middle East. His father was employed as a driller for the General Oil Company, an American firm. When a contest had been announced for the children of employees, Abdul had entered his name and had written a theme on the subject of "Why I Want to Go to America."

The winner of the contest was to be awarded a trip to the United States, where he would continue his education for one year. Abdul won the contest. In his theme, he had stated that, although he was not a Christian, he had come to be very close to his Christian teachers in the mission school. He thought that if Christians were like that, he wanted to be around them, and where else could one come to know Christians better than in America?

Abdul was a seeker, a devout Moslem. He was anxious to learn. He kept a diary while he was in the United States. The following statements are excerpts from that diary. Some of the thoughts are impressions, some lengthier discourses on his reactions to America and its people.

Under the heading "American Christianity" he wrote:

"The Christian faith is something that the Americans take for granted—almost like a birthright. Not much seems to be meant by it. They are very courteous people. They do not wish to offend anyone, so they seem to try to make their religion as inconspicuous as possible. The word "Christian" seems to mean good, or moral.

A Christian home means a clean home, but it seems to have little connection with the religion that is practiced there. The Christian students of my age are unaware of their faith. They are nice people, but the Christian doesn't seem to be any different from the non-Christian. They are so different from my missionary teachers.

"It disturbs me that the Christians in America reject the idea that other nations or faiths can have anything to offer. I don't know what they are trying to prove, but to me it sounds as though they are very insecure. I have heard myself called a heathen because I do not call Allah 'God' when I worship him. Many wrongs are committed in the name of Christ."

He says this about America as a Christian nation:

"I am much impressed with their coins. It says on them, 'In God We Trust'! How high an ideal! They salute their flag and say, "One nation, under God, indivisible, with liberty and justice for all." I wonder if they know how important that sounds? I wonder if they mean it? Patriotism is almost the religion of some people here, and the flag appears to be the symbol of their deity. I have seen the flag in their church sanctuaries. I do not understand why it is there, but it must have something to do with worship, or else why would it be displayed so prominently in a place of worship?

"They remove their hats and stand at attention when the flag goes by, but, when they curse they use the name of the Almighty and spit at the same time. Although this is godly language, the meaning is anything but godly. I do not understand this, for to me the name of Allah is not to be taken lightly.

"Christianity is more of a folkway than an ethic. To the American, it is more like going through a reducing exercise than the worship of the Almighty.

"I saw a film of a national political convention where the clergymen preached sermons in the name of prayer. One person gave the date three times in his prayer for the inauguration of one high government official. It seemed to me that he was addressing his remarks to the people, not to God. What a peculiar way to pray!

"I had heard of the problem of race in the USA, but, like so much other propaganda, I couldn't believe that it was as bad as I had been told—until I came. My dark skin qualified me to be considered a Negro, and my passport meant nothing to them. I can't be sure that it was prejudice, but I had to wait for two hours to be fed one day. It may be that this is a custom reserved for foreign guests, and it may indicate the great care with which the meal was being prepared, but the food was cold when I was served.

"I read an article written by a Christian saying that people should have the freedom to discriminate.

"I used to be afraid of war in the Sheikdom. I had heard of bomb tests and of the talk of war, but I thought that in this great and powerful Christian land there would be no such fear. I was wrong. I don't know why they are so afraid. They have so much power—and tanks and guns and bombs.

"They were angry because another big country was contaminating the air with radiation. They insisted that if they did it, it was all right, because they were a Christian country. I wonder if it hurts more for a Christian to die than for the heathen? I have been taught that Allah cares for all people, not just the Christian,

"I heard about a man named John Birch. I never saw him while I was there and I have him confused with the group called Ku Klux Klan. I understand that it is a Christian organization too. It frightens me."

Here are his impressions of the Christian church:

"Great churches, so big you can hardly see the top of the steeple, great numbers of people, much money. Methodist church alone numbers ten million people.

"They are doing great things in those churches, exciting things. And they are also doing little things in big ways. There is much concern about which translation of the Bible to use. They have church fairs. People spend weeks working for them. The proceeds are divided between preparations for the fair for the next year and buying dish towels for the ladies' bridge group that meets there weekly.

"They have a trading stamp club that meets every two weeks to put stamps in books. They have dessert and are going to buy a portable outdoor grille for summer parties. They have programs using free films on forestry, how diamonds are mined, and the many practical uses of linseed oil. I don't understand how this related to the church, but one of the nice ladies told me it keeps her from being bored and helps to bring in the Kingdom of God.

"I am confused. They send letters to congressmen about race questions in South Africa, but they won't allow Negroes to come to their churches.

"They have interesting classes for high school students on running the mimeograph machine and how to make apple butter.

"It is interesting the way the church is a community center—almost like a country club, except it is easier for most people to get into it.

"When I go to their church, I can't tell whether they are worshipping the minister or God. The minister keeps referring to what he has done for people.

"It is my impression, although I wouldn't want them to know this, that the minister wants to be liked much more than he wants to interpret the will of God. He is a nice man, he doesn't offend anyone, and the church seems to like him; he keeps them on an even keel. No dissension.

"At the bottom of each church bulletin, he has written 'The Church of Optimism.' He often cautions his people not to rock the boat. What a strange phrase. He is such a nice man, not very effective, but nice."

Under the section titled "Christian College" he says:

"I went to a Christian college; it was most interesting.

"I could tell it was a Christian school—they advertise it in their bulletin—and they have signs on cornerstones. The name Wesley has something to do with it. One of the students told me that Wesley had been a member of their Board of Trustees, that he had been a big publisher and had left his money to start colleges that would bear his name. The student thought he was a Presbyterian minister, on a religious kick, whatever he meant by that.

"I asked some students about Christianity on campus and they laughed at me—they were so friendly. I guess my accent made it hard for them to understand what I meant! So I didn't ask again.

"I was in a student eating place and overheard students in a discussion. One said 'Religion is for the misfits,' and one told in great detail of a roommate of his who used to go to church every Sunday morning. He stopped finally, because the men in the house made such fun of him. He indicated that any thinking students wouldn't go near a church unless his parents were on the campus.

"I asked about a quaint custom they have of going to chapel in the middle of the week. They doubled up with laughter and mentioned something about the best time of day to sleep, even in those cramped seats. One of the men spoke of the reverse metamorphosis that takes place—when a human being becomes an animal as soon as he steps inside the chapel door. He didn't tell me what he meant by that.

"I did get in on a bull session, I didn't know what they meant before. Most of it dealt with whether they should use crepe paper or aluminum foil to decorate the nine-foot tall bunny for their party they were going to call Playboy Away from Home. The men wondered whether the dean of women would find out about the kind of costumes the girls would wear. I don't know what they meant, but they laughed a lot.

"They talked of two other things: their conquests of women, and ten ways to spike punch without detection. There was a lot of talk around the Christian campus about some exercise they were doing—they called it the Twist. It may have come from a course in comparative religions and been a form of Yoga.

"They have clubs there. They advertise them as Christian clubs, but one of the men said that was only in the ritual and no one paid any attention to it. It was mostly for the benefit of the alumni and the trustees and administration of the college.

"The value of the club was the exam file system and the fact that food was cheaper than at the college.

"I have mixed feelings about the school, and the church, and the country. I like them, their openness, their friendship (most of the time), their talking and singing and boisterous behavior, their carefree attitude about problems of the world that concern us in the Middle East.

"But I can't understand how they can call all of these things Christian. It may be that I have the wrong idea, but my missionary friend led me to believe that things were different in a Christian land."

Abdul went home to his Bedouin life. He went back to the mission school and practiced a different kind of faith.

Scripture — MATTHEW 23:l-7a, llb-15, 23-24, 27-32, 37-38

Jesus then addressed the people and his disciples in these words: The doctors of the law and the Pharisees sit in the chair of Moses; therefore do what they tell you; pay attention to their words. But do not follow their practices; for they say one thing and do another. They make heavy packs and pile them on men's shoulders, but will not raise a finger to lift the load themselves. Whatever they do is done for show. They go about with Morocco-bound prayer books and wear proper black garments; they like to have places of honor at feasts and the front pews in churches, to be greeted respectfully in the street, and to be addressed as 'leaders.'

The greatest among you must be your servant, for whoever exalts himself will be humbled; and whoever humbles himself will be exalted.

Alas for you, community leaders and Christians, hypocrites that you are! You shut the door of the kingdom of Heaven in men's faces; you do not enter yourselves, and when others are entering, you stop them.

Alas for you, community leaders and Christians, hypocrites! You travel over sea and land to win one convert; and when you have won him you make him twice as fit for hell as you are yourselves.

Alas for you, community leaders, Christians, hypocrites! You pay tithes of mint and dill and cumin; but you have overlooked the weightier demands of the law, justice, mercy and good faith. It is these you should have practiced, without neglecting the others. Blind guides! You strain off a gnat, yet gulp down a camel!

Alas for you, community leaders, Christians, hypocrites! You are like tombs covered with whitewash; they look well from outside, but inside they are full of dead men's bones and all kinds of filth. So it is with you: Outside you look like honest men, but inside you are brim-full of hypocrisy and crime.

O Jerusalem, Jerusalem, the city that murders the prophets and stones the messenger sent to her! How often have I longed to gather your children, as a hen gathers her brood under wings, but you would not let me. Look, look, there is your temple, forsaken by God!

I Forgot Her Name

1985

(Lines from a blushing, embarrassed, but friendly college-type chaplain. A student repaid a loan and I forgot her name.)

> *January 15, 1985*
> *Ms. Mary Moynihan*
> *Box 0504*
> *'Twas a dark day for the chaplain*
> *'Twas a time of deep remorse*
> *For Mary came with greenbacks*
> *(He forgot her name, of course).*
>
> *Now pride is what we've got here*
> *And promises, and such*
> *Remember when he said to you*
> *"I won't forget" (not much!)*
>
> *If only you would stop by*
> *For two days, that's my plan*
> *So weary eyes could get a fix*
> *On Mary Moynihan.*
>
> *I know I said, "I'll not forget,*
> *Just try me and you'll see."*

But now I guess I must confess
I'm not what I claim to be.

But give me 10 more times (at least)
Perhaps an even twenty
I'm sure before you graduate
I'll know your name, a-plenty.

A Retirement Party

Spring 1988: A "thank you" for a surprise retirement "happening" at the Peace and Justice House

> 'Twas the night before Thursday in P&J House
> Not a creature was stirring, not even my spouse.
> The parlor was empty, the halls were all silent
> All creatures seemed absent, (they're normally violent!)
> When back near the kitchen a few squeals could be heard
> Lotsa moaning and scratching, I thought 'twas a bird.
> When what to my wandering eyes did appear
> But a thousand conspirators with huge flapping ears.
> Their giggles, how merry! Their shouting, in chorus
> Full tilt, let me have it, of cour-us, of cour-us.
>
> The light from the kitchen, the hall and the eatery
> 'Most blinded old eyes, by that time getting watery.
>
> The cameras were clicking, the bands in fine fettle
> Were playing my tune on a kettle of metal.
>
> The table was covered with goodies galore
> It moaned from the weight of what was in store.
>
> For locusts did swarm ere they pulled out of sight
> Celebration to all, and to all a good flight.

So thanks to the crew that inhabits your house
Thanks to free-loaders (including my spouse).

Thanks for inviting my friends and my neighbors
To a dandy s'prise party, you did me great favors.

You showed such affection, I simply can't stand it
'Twill always be 'membered by Chappy (the bandit)!

Thanks to You, It Worked

May 8, 1988: Commencement

The following was sent to janitors, cooks, dishwashers, and others in thanks for their part in Commencement.

> *The chairs have gone, the P.A.'s quiet,*
> *The food's been et, back to our diet.*
> *It's 'bout that time to thank the thankees,*
> *Some are Rebels, some are Yankees.*
> *Some are Pittsburgh Pirates fans,*
> *Some have made outlandish plans*
> *To 'scape th'environs of this fine city,*
> *To sleep in late, get lookin' pretty.*
> *To claim the sunshine, smell the roses,*
> *To cycle bikes, to prance on toeses*
> *T'enjoy a time of relaxation*
> *From meeting folks at airplane stations.*
> *To slow down some and hear the chillen*
> *Come home from school, so very willin'*
> *As you relax from times of pressure,*
> *Accept my thanks, you are a treasure!*
> *By any measure you made things happen,*
> *You prepped the campus, for you we're clappin'.*
> *You typed the lists, you set the tables,*
> *You filled the cups; your skills are fabled.*

You pushed the buttons, filled balloons,
Swept the walks, worked way past noon.
You cleaned the carpets, made up beds,
Put up signs of Blacks and Reds.
You lined up students late on Sunday,
Picked up caps, thrown all a-sundry.
You tinkered with the P.A. soundings,
Kept out squeaks, (now that's astounding!)
Your detailed tasks made us look dandy,
So thanks for that; you're mighty handy!
Thanks for leading in the students,
And for always showing prudence.
Thanks for sporting regalia's brightness,
Sorry 'bout the gowns' too tightness!
Sorry If I left out any,
Or pleased too few or hurt too many.
Thanks for things I can't remember,
(I'll recall them, come December!)
Thanks for doing necessaries,
Thank you sixteen thousand verys!

When Did We See You?

[Undated manuscript.]

Emmanuel was a bright young man. He was the hope of his village in a newly independent nation in central Africa. He had been the first to read and write in his family. How proud they were of him. He had gone to the mission school and had to walk or ride his donkey three miles each way to attend class. He was not able to work because of his school, so the family was somewhat hard-pressed financially. But they didn't complain, because Emmanuel obviously was going to make a name for his nation.

Well, it wasn't impossible. When had such talent been seen before? Even the legendary people in his tribe had never possessed the skills that he did. He had never performed miracles, but his ability to read and write had meant the difference between the village having good crops and its having the customary low yield that most small farms had in his vicinity.

But Emmanuel had read, and he had talked with the agricultural workers at the mission station, and he had taken samples of the soil to the lab and had learned of its needing fertilizer and of crop rotation and of special planting techniques to make the best use of the contours of the land. He was becoming a legend in his own time—and people knew that their investment in his education would be an investment in their nation's future, and they were glad to do it.

Family and friends spoke with government officials about Emmanuel, so that when the time came for him to learn a trade, he was called into the office of the government's representative and offered financial help to go wherever he could be accepted for university training. Unfortunately, the frequency of strikes at the university in the nation's capital had meant that ongoing education was hazardous, and, besides, so many were already enrolled there that space in classes was at a premium, and, with the crowded conditions because of refugees coming from Uganda, there was not likely to be a place for him to live in the city near the university.

Emmanuel's teacher at the mission school suggested that should he not be able to go to the government university, he might want to consider going to her college in the United States. She felt that the officials there would help make some financial aid available and he could work once the language problem was resolved and his courses were going well.

Emmanuel was most excited about the prospects of traveling by plane, for he had never been far from his village, much less flown in an airplane. He had seen them in the sky on their way to the capital, but had never been close to one.

Since the autumn term began within a few months, plans had to be worked on quickly. Emmanuel's teacher made several phone calls to her alma mater and was able to secure the promise of the first year's room, board, and tuition in exchange for some tutorial work that Emmanuel might give to French students. Emmanuel's main languages were three local dialects, so limited in their usage that they had never been written down, but his education had been in French, the language of all trade and education in his country. He also was fluent in Swahili and was a quick learner, so there was little doubt that he could pick up English quickly.

From the day of his acceptance until he took the plane three months later, he spent part of every day in the slow process of learning to communicate in English with his teacher. The strange "th" sounds could not be mastered, and the curious way of pronouncing the letter *r* was hard for him. But his brightness and his eagerness to learn helped him to know enough English that his sponsors were sure that he would not have too many problems once he was immersed in his new language.

As the time approached for him to leave for the new world, he became more and more concerned about how he would adjust to his new surroundings. Would people know of his tribe's traditions? But how couldn't they? Everyone knew that at the time of marriage the wife's family is given cows or goats and, naturally, everyone knew that many animals are taboo and that lizards are never to be harmed because they were holy. And since Emmanuel had always known that special attention would be paid to what he said because he was the first-born son, he was confident that, even if other folkways of his people were not followed in the new world, certainly they would give him special attention because of the position that he held in his family and in his tribe. But he wasn't sure how that difference would be evidenced.

His family could hardly bear the thought of his being away for such a long time. Four years might not seem such a great length of time to some people, but to people from his area, where life expectancy was 45 years, it could mean one-tenth of one's lifetime that he would be in the new world! The whole week before he left, his family held a continuous festival both honoring him and grieving for his imminent departure. The youths of the village played their drums and danced late into the night, but the elders poured ashes over their heads and cried, not always softly, for most of them knew they would never see Emmanuel again.

His uncle's donkey cart was his transportation to the capital, where he spent the night with a cousin, and the next day he was driven to the airport in an open bus, the seats of which were long boards running the width of the bus and holding considerably more people than one would expect could fit into a bus.

The Air France plane was the largest vehicle he had seen in his lifetime and, although he had read about planes and knew the principles of physics that explained how flight worked, it was hard for him to believe that such a heavy object would ever be able to fly and to think that he would soon be in a country where almost everyone flew and where other wonders were simply commonplace. What an exciting day this was, and what a sad day, and what a concerning day, and what a bewildering day. It was too much for him. He felt sick.

The plane ride was a disaster for him. He couldn't stretch out. He couldn't overcome his headache. His feet swelled when he took his shoes off and he couldn't get the shoes on again without discomfort. When the plane landed in the Canary Islands, he misunderstood and thought that he was in America only to find that this was a refueling stop and that the trip was only one-quarter over. The film that they showed on the plane was the kind that he had never been permitted to watch. It dealt with murder and rape and prostitution, and he had never been allowed to talk about those subjects, much less see them in color and while using those earphones that made him feel surrounded by immorality.

He couldn't sleep, and he was sick and worried and confused, and wasn't sure whether the sun should be rising or setting. They kept telling him to change the hour on his watch. He knew about time zones, but hadn't realized how disorienting it would be to have eaten breakfast a few hours ago and realize that it was still breakfast time again on the ground beneath him. It was like living in a never-never land.

He found, for instance, that his tribe's practice of never looking in the eyes of a person you met was viewed as a sign of timidity by the Americans. He was showing proper respect for them by not appearing to threaten them by direct eye contact. They took this as a sign of weakness and submission. When they shook hands, it was as if they wanted to wrestle with you or test your strength, but his custom was to present a gentle hand, showing no hostility or anger, but they only took it as a sign of an effeminate person and teased him about it.

He was particularly disturbed that people who were supposed to be his helpers—the faculty advisors, residence counselors, and dormitory student assistants—all said that they would help him, but they never did. All they did was talk to him about the various alternatives and options open to him and never told him which was best for him. It was such a different system. How could he choose from among all of them when he didn't understand any of them or at least feel comfortable with any of them?

In his village, his family made his decisions, the way it should be. Those who had lived longer knew more about the implications of a bad choice. They had lived through it. They were best prepared to tell him what to do. Now everyone was saying "It's your choice," and his elders wouldn't tell him. They said he should learn to do these things and that he would grow by doing it. How strange. How wrong. Surely they were abdicating their responsibility. It looked to him as though they weren't very good counselors if they couldn't tell people what to do or how to solve their problems.

Then someone told him that he smelled, and the resident counselor and his faculty advisor took him aside on two different occasions to tell him that he needed to take better care of his hygiene. What they really meant was he should wash more often. What they didn't know was that he was a very clean person but that in his village water was so scarce and so hard to get that everyone was very careful not to waste it; baths were taken less often and water used with great care. Over here people let the tap water run, sometimes for over an hour, with no one using it, simply because they were too careless to turn it off.

Now, he thought, who is the offender, the person who has body odor or the person who misuses the earth's resources? Surely they could see the difference! But they didn't. All they knew was that Emmanuel smelled and that it was hard to relate to him. They gave him all kinds of suggestions concerning deodorants that he could use. They must have been convinced that such application would make it easier to live close to him, but he was convinced that the chemicals used in the deodorant would be harmful to his body and would outweigh the advantages of smelling good.

Food was a problem for Emmanuel. At first, he felt as though he was at a feast at every meal, for the cafeteria had unlimited quantities of food for him—everyday things that he might have had in his village once in several years—but here they were a regular part of his diet. He could have all manner of soft drinks, all the ice cream he desired, fresh butter, and peanut-butter—how he liked that—and all that he wanted. But before long, he found that he seldom had rice, that he never had cassava, that he only had one kind of banana instead of the 15 varieties at home. They had never heard of foo-foo—his basic food at home. When he told them what it was like, one of the students mentioned that he had been on a work camp in a neighboring country and had eaten it often, and that it looked and tasted like library paste. They all laughed, but Emmanuel felt ill at ease with such talk.

It had been completely dark outside the plane for a long time when suddenly there were hundreds of lights, no thousands, no it was almost as if a blanket of lights were beneath the plane. It was New York. The plane circled for a long time waiting to land and finally it did.

As he looked back on that experience, it was one he never wanted to live through again. It seemed as though all the passengers had a friend or relative meeting them—all except Emmanuel. Everyone knew what papers to have ready except Emmanuel. Everyone knew which exit to go through, which arrows to follow, how to approach official-looking people to ask what one should do about spending the night, what to do if one had missed the connecting plane, where to change money, how to use a telephone, where one could wash up, where one would find the packages containing his clothes.

No one seemed to care and everyone was busy. They didn't walk, they ran. They were scowling. This was the New World and no one was smiling! Finally, someone who had been on the plane with him and who had been in the Peace Corps in a country next to his, spoke to Emmanuel, realizing that things were not well. He spent the next hour-and-a-half with him and led him through the necessary steps at the airport. He also took him to the YMCA hotel in the city and arranged to help him the next morning. What a difference it meant knowing someone who cared and who must have sensed the confusion in Emmanuel's mind.

With his new friend's help, he made reservations on a plane to get him to college and that afternoon arrived at a much smaller airport, where a student driver with a large college sign met him. How wonderful to be expected and to be wanted. He wanted to cry but knew how embarrassed people would be, so held his tears in check.

He was taken to a wonderful city, large by his standards, but small, according to the student. It was a "county seat town," whatever that meant, and was to be his home for the next four years.

He went to the dormitory—it looked very new—and was helped with his luggage on the elevator and up to his room. He couldn't imagine having an elevator in his own building. (He was later to spend an inordinate amount of time riding the elevator up and down, often helping other arriving students so he could have some excuse to push the buttons and experience the sensation of rising or falling in that metal cage.) He wondered why students living in a new building didn't take better care of it. The main entrance showed signs of a water fight the night before. Several lamps were broken and three window panes were shattered in the lobby. How could people live this way?

He hadn't expected to be a curiosity, but he was. The American students were very breezy about the way they greeted him, asking him if he had elephants or lions at home and if he rode to school on a bullock. What he wouldn't tell them was that he usually did ride to school on his donkey, but he knew that they would make fun of him and his people if he told them that.

He became overpowered by the sea of white faces. He had nothing against whites as long as they weren't acting like colonialists. But having no other African friends who were students there and having to find friends among the whites was very complicated; he wasn't sure how to go about it.

Emmanuel went to many of the students' social gatherings and was surprised to find that alcohol was the common bond among them. One seldom scheduled a recreational event without planning on plenty to drink. He knew that this happened in his country, although seldom in his village. He knew that some people who could afford it drank too much and sometimes had to go the hospital and sometimes never came back. But, when so many drank so much and had enough money to pay for more, he felt out of place and didn't like the feeling when being friends with them meant having to drink with them. For some of the students it was almost a condition for friendship and it seemed to him they drank not to enjoy the beverage, but to get drunk. What were they running from? Why were they trying to escape? They talked a great deal about America being the best country in the world and that their system of free enterprise was so valued, yet they seemed to try to get away from so much of that same life by being drunk. He heard stories of how many of the students were likely to become alcoholics, but they scoffed at such a suggestion and said that he had been reading too many conservative publications.

After some months among his new American friends, he decided that if he was going to live among Americans he would try to do what they did. So he began to drink and, later, encouraged by some of his friends, he entered contests to see who could drink the most. One time he drank so much that he lost awareness of where he was. He propositioned a co-ed, something he would never have done sober, and he joined a friend who set off three fire extinguishers in the dormitory. When he was caught, his American friend denied any involvement in it, and he was required to pay the full fine of $50, which he could not afford at the time. That was as much as his father sometimes earned in five months at home. The student who had encouraged his drinking and who had started the fire extinguisher raid made fun of his predicament and continued to absolve himself of any responsibility.

Coming from a tropical climate made him unprepared for the severity of the winter. His clothing was fine for the autumn but hardly warm enough for the below-zero temperature that the campus was experiencing. His host family in the community was annoyed with his having been charged with drunken behavior by the student court and refused to continue to help him. He had no more money to buy warm clothing so often he went to class wearing several layers of clothing, including his pajamas, two shirts, three sweaters and his suit jacket. He looked odd, and people often commented on his new style but never offered to help him secure warm clothing.

One evening, he and another student were wrestling playfully in the dormitory corridor. The playfulness changed into ugliness when the American refused to release a particularly painful head-lock, and Emmanuel, only after begging him to stop, broke the grip by biting the wrist of the student and breaking the skin. It was a free-for-all after that, with 15 minutes of angry blows. Emmanuel was used to fighting with his feet and threw his body at the student, landing a very painful kick with one foot but with the other shattering the plate glass at the top of the fire door in the hall. That stopped the fight, but the gash on his ankle sent Emmanuel to the hospital, where the pieces of glass had to be removed from the wound and 20 stitches taken. He was hospitalized for four days while the student courts were trying him *in absentia* for his dormitory fighting and breaking a very expensive door.

His host family sent him a card but didn't go to see him because they knew what a private person he was and how he might feel ill at ease with Americans stopping to see him after he had been humiliated.

Dormitory friends were angry because although Emmanuel paid the bulk of the charges for the door, the cost was so high that each student on the corridor had to pay for part of it, the reasoning being that they could have stopped the fight before it became so bad. They weren't about to visit the person who had made them pay $4 each.

The chaplain couldn't see him because he was away at a conference learning how to deal with students facing crises. Emmanuel's instructors had committee meetings and tennis tournaments, and the faculty club met one of the nights he was there. Besides, why single him out when they never went to see other students? After all, that was the democratic way, wasn't it?

By the end of the winter term Emmanuel was tired—tired of trying to become Americanized, tired of being the one to reach out to make the concessions, to speak in a language other than his own. He began to be more vocal against the foreign policy of America, taking the position of his socialist country's leader, who was particularly angry with U.S. policy. Emmanuel helped organize protest meetings that called into question some of the practices of America, especially those dealing with the sale of military arms to dictatorial countries and those that held the black population down.

When the immigration authorities made their regular visit to the campus, one of the deans reported Emmanuel as being an alien who should be investigated. When the Immigration and Naturalization Service called him in, he became aware of how hard it would be for him to stay and how much he really wanted to leave. He stopped going to classes, kept to his room in the dormitory, would not answer the telephone, refused to eat American food, lost weight, and retreated from almost all social contact.

And so he left to go back home, where he belonged, where he was needed, where he was somebody. He was taken to the airport by the dean of students, who talked at length to him about his reasons for unhappy experiences at the university. Emmanuel's last comment as he left for the airport gate was, "Where were you when I needed you?"

Matthew 25:31-40

Lord, when did we see you in the person of the Iranian students in Delaware, who are scared, who can't go home, who don't have the money to stay here, who can't demonstrate or voice complaints the way they might, lest they be sent away by immigration?

Lord, when did we see you in the person of the husband whose marriage is falling apart, whose children have turned against him, and whose employer is about to fire him because of the stories that he has heard about him?

Lord, when did we see you in the woman who is a talented orchestra conductor, whose skills are not measured by her talents, but by her attractiveness, or lack of it, and who is limited in how far she can go because few major orchestras have ever had women conductors?

Lord, when did we see you in the person of the delinquent boy, who has never had a home where he belonged, who has been passed from family to family, each one rejecting him because he cannot conform to their standard of what a boy should be?

Lord, when did we see you?

Get off My Back, Lord

[Undated manuscript]

Get off my back, Lord. Since when did my profession of belief in you, in the Christian church, mean that I had to take so many stands?

Why must I separate myself from my friends, from my parents, from my family, from those I love the most, because of issues on which we disagree?

I can't win. When I take a stand, I'm hounded by those who don't like it; when I don't take a stand, I'm hounded by those who believe that I should.

I want to party it up. I want to go to dances and open houses. I want to play my party games. I want to organize a huge love-in. I want to take off and do my thing.

I don't want to be involved in this damnable war. I don't want to read about the fighting. I don't want to hear the gory details. I don't want to see the pictures of the bodies being carted away like so much refuse. I don't want to have the value of life determined by whether or not a person is a communist. I don't want to make the distinction in life between a capitalist from the West—whose face is white and whose belief is Protestant—who is automatically good, and the peasant who can't have a voice in his own government and who is automatically bad. I don't want to be confronted with the war day after day.

I don't want to have my friends go off to war. I want them to be able to make the kinds of career choices that others have made in more normal times. I want people to be able to decide what they will die for. Lord, why do I have to decide if my government is telling me the truth? Why must I take the initiative to be a promoter of unpopular causes? Why can't I just escape, get away from all these problems? Why can't I just go fishing, just read a quiet book, one that will end up with everyone loving everyone else? I hear the problems on the radio. I watch them on TV.

I see them at the flicks. I talk about them with my friends and there seems to be no way out.

Stop pressuring me, Lord. Knock off all this involvement business and let me live my life, let me make my felt banners, and let my hang-ups be in making nooses, and let me have my chuckles for the day and comment on no noose being good noose. Get off my back, and get back up there on the gallows, where you belong, where you can't involve me. Get back up there on your pretty cross, the one that is gold plated, the one that cost lots of money. Get up there and be crucified by Romans with the compliance of Jews so I can blame anyone else but myself. Don't get me involved in being responsible for your death. I'm clean, I'm pure, I'm not involved.

I want my religion to be neat, compact, foldable, bendable. I want to be able to hold it in front of me. I want to be able to see it, to know where I can put it when I'm not using it. I want to be able to file it, to store it, to pack it away, to cart it out when it is appropriate. I want to define it, label it. I want to date it, attribute it to people, but please, don't confuse me with having to decide if it fits into my life, or if it is really Christian, or if it is relevant.

I've got enough problems of my own. I've got a family. I've got a house to pay for. I've got a board of trustees to please, a bishop to agree with me, a tradition to maintain. Don't make me be relevant, too.

I want to live in peace, and I can have peace if you'll only stay in Jerusalem or Bethlehem or Nazareth or Galilee, where you belong. Stay with the camels and the goatherds. Stay with King James English. Stay with Sunday school maps of Old Testament days. Stay with Pauline travels. Stay with the early martyrs but don't go mucking about with my life and with my nation. As long as what you had to say applied hard and often to fishermen and to tax collectors and to Pharisees and publicans, that was all right, but when you begin to call these people college students and homemakers and secretaries and deans and chaplains, watch out. You are making this too close to home, and I'm not about to give up my freedom and get out of my nice warm groove for some trumped-up program for helping some poor little idiot of a brown man in some Asian country whose name I can hardly pronounce, much less whose language and customs I can understand.

Go back to your prayers on the Mount of Olives, pray in Aramaic or Hebrew, translate it into Greek and Latin, but don't put it into my idiom because then you're pushing me, and I've got enough people pushing me just now, thanks so very much.

Keep your piety old fashioned and irrelevant. Speak to Amos. Let justice roll down like a mighty stream but let it be the justice of Amos' day. I can dig that slavery bit. I'm not about to go out and buy me a slave. I can abide not having more than one wife and I'm not planning to abandon my children because four out of five of them happen to be girls, who are going to cost me much more and are likely to earn less than if they were boys. I dig that.

But if you are going to spout off about how nothing has changed, that the problems are the same or may even be worse, if you aren't going to let me have my ideas that things are much better now than they used to be, then count me out. If you aren't going to ever let me have this much satisfaction, then I'm not sure I want any part of your movement and, to prove it, I'm going to stay away from your Sunday morning festivities. I'm not going to sing your hymns and I'm not going to give any money for your cause.

Don't think you can attach strings to your belief. Don't think that you can get me to live by your absurd standards. After all, what practical man ever heard of turning the other cheek? Whoever heard of giving one's coat away? Whoever heard of loving an enemy? No wonder they nailed you to a couple of pieces of wood. You obviously were at least off your rocker and at most were a perpetrator of some kind of a fantastic hoax.

If I want to judge people, I'm going to do it. If I want to live according to my own illusions, then let me, but let them be my illusions, not yours.

If I want to live my fat, happy self-centered life, then you are not going to stop that. So it may be wrong, but at least it is honest. Get off my back, Lord—and leave me alone.

Let me be free of this intangible something that hangs on. I can't stand those cries in the night. I can't stand thrashing about in my sleep. I can't stand waking up in the morning feeling that something is wrong.

Get off me. Stop being my conscience. Don't lean on me anymore. Why should I be concerned about the ghettos in Philadelphia and Chicago? What affair is it of mine if the rats have taken over the slums? Let the landlords fight that out with the tenants. Let the social workers press their charges. Let the poverty program publicize that. Let the VISTA volunteers preach their sermons. And leave me alone to refinish my antique bureaus and re-cane the old rocking chair in the shed.

I work hard at my office. I answer the crank mail and placate my secretary. I speak kind words to the elevator operator and I even gave him a Christmas tip. Now what else am I supposed to do? Rent a hall, so he can tell the world about the inequities between his salary scale and mine?

Stop bugging me with that "do unto others" bit. I heard enough of that in Sunday school and that was only because I was gullible then. Now I am a man of the world and am not as easily taken in with your pious double talk of doing good for the world. The world just doesn't care. You do good for it and it slaps you down. You stop to help a person who has been seriously injured, and you end up with a law suit on your hands for having hurt the person you were trying to help.

I'm fed up to my ears with this bit about race. I'm tired of feeling guilty, tired of having to eat humble pie, tired of having the problem as big or bigger now than it was before we had any of the civil rights legislation. Why is it my problem? Who appointed me the bearer of the world's problems?

Leave me alone. I don't want to have to face up to what we are spending in our futile race to the moon. I don't want to see the comparative figures of our funding of poverty programs and our funding of war efforts.

I want to wave a flag. I want to have tears in my eyes when the band plays the national anthem. I want to be proud of those who are fighting for my country all over the world, but I find it increasingly difficult to do that. I can't just say, "It's my country, therefore it is right." I can't just live without thinking and I can't let others do my thinking for me, even if those people are supposed to be the best leaders that we have. What if they are wrong and I am right? What happens then?

Why me, Lord, why me? Why not some other guy who isn't thrown by this involvement bit? What have I done that I should be bugged by this? Why does my thing have to mean being tied up with all these issues? Who says so? Who put me on the mailing list of all the conscience causes? Why do I have to defend all the defenseless? Why do I have to espouse all the causes that others don't or won't or can't espouse?

Why can't things be simple, the way they used to be? Why can't I just vote at election time instead of having to campaign and donate funds and ring doorbells for my candidate? Why does ability imply responsibility? Why must I feel responsible when my government says or does something that I cannot support? Why do I have to serve on one more church committee when I don't have the time to get my work done now?

Leave me alone. Let me be. Turn off your wavelength to my receiver. Get out of my life and let me vegetate. Let me think my thoughts, dream my private dreams, build my empires, live in my split-level house next to my golfing buddies. I'm not sure I'm being honest with you, Lord. I'm not sure what I want, but I certainly know what I don't want, I don't want to be in so much turmoil, to be torn apart by the many claims of my time, my hands, my life.

I want what I do to be purposive, to have meaning. I want (although it doesn't often happen) to be able to sit down after work and realize that something good happened that day. I don't want to be my brother's keeper, but I would very much like to be my brother's brother.

I want the message and meaning of my religion to make sense. I want to strip away from it the poetic language of another era that has little if any meaning for me and make it speak to me in words that I can understand. I want the virility of the faith to sound out. I want the strength and excitement of being a Christian to be in evidence. I want the healing, not the sickening side of the faith to show. I'd like to put away the statements of the church that separate people from me and from the Christ and emphasize what Christianity is all about, after all. I deny that this faith is a series of prohibitions and rules and laws. I affirm that it is the freedom to choose, the freedom to become, the freedom to live, creatively and openly.

It means that in spite of all that seems to be falling apart at the seams, there is hope. It means that even in the midst of holocaust there is peace. But it is a restless peace that will come for me best if I get going and do something about it.

You Atheist

[Undated manuscript.]

You, who are angry at having the spotlight turned on yourself, the very spotlight you seek to throw on others.

YOU ARE ACCEPTED.

You, whose last wish is to be thought of as a child of God.

You, whose only purpose in being here this evening is to satisfy your wife who has wrung a promise from you to go to church during Lent.

You, who find it hard to stomach religion in any form.

You are loved by God perhaps more than others, for

You are searching for meaning while many of us are not.

Your atheism is accepted by the one against whom you seek to vent your spleen.

You are accepted, by the very God you so earnestly have separated yourself from.

Your rejection is accepted.

Your strength is accepted.

Your rebellion is accepted and valued.

You, Judas, you, who betrays a confidence.

You, who can be bought.

You, who can turn love into mockery

You, who use people for gain.

You, who cannot even trust yourself.

YOU ARE ACCEPTED.

You, who have been taught to love people and use things but end up using people and loving things.

YOU ARE ACCEPTED.

You, who are trying but getting nowhere.

You, who are flunking, in school, in marriage, in life.

You, who find no reason for living, no meaning in being here.

YOU ARE ACCEPTED

You, who hate your parents but don't express it.

You, who cheated in the exam this morning.

You, who spoke in anger to the one you love.

You, who fear the unknown and can't stand uncertainty.

YOU ARE ACCEPTED.

You, who just learned that your father has incurable cancer.

You, who hate.

You, whose mother died before you could reach her.

You, to whom fear is a constant companion.

You, obsessed with gaining wealth and fame.

You, obsessed by defeating your roommate in grade point average.

You, obssessed by a God who makes you a fanatic.

YOU ARE ACCEPTED.

You are loved. You are a child of God. You are God's creation. Go, and the acceptance of God be felt by you.

Voices from the Chapel Walls

May 15, 1988

MICAH 6:8, I SAMUEL 3:1-10, HEBREWS 12:1-2

"As for us, we have this large crowd of witnesses around us. So, then, let us rid ourselves of everything that gets in the way and of the sin which holds on to us so tightly, and let us run with determination the race that lies before us. Speak, Lord, for your servant is listening."

It seems appropriate on Alumni Weekend to speak of the people and the voices that we remember from earlier days at Ohio Wesleyan—the Walkers, the Rices, the Spencers, the Arnesons, the Davieses, the Edwardses, the Eastons, and on and on. These, and others like them, are the people, the voices that have influenced thousands of Ohio Wesleyan students.

Samuel thought that it was Eli who called to him, but learned that it was God, so he said, "Speak, Lord, for your servant is listening." Joan of Arc, the Maid of Orleans, heard voices, and they helped to direct her life.

We raise questions about the stability of some folk who hear voices. Oral Roberts has seen visions of a 900-foot Jesus who told him to build a medical center. Later he claims to have communicated with God about raising several millions of dollars or he would be called home.

The voices to which I refer, however, are not those to raise funds or those to guide an army, but are the voices that come from printed material and from the greats, near greats, and common greats among us who say and write things that need to be remembered.

For me, some of these voices are the signs, posters, and sayings that have hung on the chapel walls here and in the Memorial Union Chapel and the Chaplain's Office. These voices speak to the most pressing issues of their and our day. They are heavy; they are light. They are world-shaking, and they are humorous. They prick the bubbles of our more pompous ideas and they remind us of crusades and the needs of their time and our time. They speak for themselves. They urge a concern for causes and for individuals; they urge sanity at a time of idiocy. They are sometimes picture words, telling more with a photo than by language.

In my office, there is a picture of Jacques Cousteau, whose plea to save sea animals and the fish of the oceans and whose concern for the future of the oceans may save them.

There is Martin Luther King Jr., who said, "Peace is not the absence of tension, but the presence of justice."

There is Martin Luther, who said, "Even if I knew certainly the world could end tomorrow, I would plant an apple tree today."

Norman Cousins wrote: "Death is not the greatest loss in life. The greatest loss is what dies inside us while we live. The unbearable tragedy is to live without dignity or sensitivity."

There is a picture of graffiti on a city wall that reads, "Reporter: 'Mr. Gandhi, what do you think of Western civilization?' Gandhi: 'I think it would be a good idea.'"

There is a picture of Nkosinathi Qunta, a South African young man who lived in our home for a year and who has died, either because of a snake bite or because his country wanted him to die.

There is Ellen Kuzwayo, a South African author and recent speaker at Ohio Wesleyan. She pleads for justice in her homeland. There is a hungry child from Bangladesh who is begging for food, with a rice bowl in her outstretched hand.

There is the Women's International League for Peace and Friendship whose poster reads: "It will be a great day when our schools get all the money they need and the Air Force has to hold a bake sale to buy a bomber."

There is the Aldous Huxley quotation: "We are caught between being unloving critics and uncritical lovers."

A Mark Twain sign says, "Always do right. This will gratify some people and astonish the rest."

Gandhi said, "I do not want my house to be walled on all sides and my windows to be stuffed. I want the culture of all lands to be blown about my house as freely as possible."

John Wesley, after whom this University is named, said, "Let us unite the two so long divided: knowledge and vital piety."

Robert McAfee Brown says, "You are called upon to be who you are, where you are; not to be somebody else somewhere else." This has had particular significance for me. In 1969, I agreed to take a position in Nashville, but I wasn't sure that I really wanted to make the change. While wrestling with this decision, I dreamed that a space ship landed and I was invited inside. I was told that the ship would take me to the most wonderful place in the world and that I would really like where we were to land. When we did land, the doors were opened, I walked outside, and there it was: Delaware, Ohio! The poster that says, "Bloom where you are planted" has been a favorite of mine ever since.

"If we have love in our hearts, disagreement will do us no harm. If we do not have love in our hearts, agreement will do us no good."

"Sexism is a subtle disease."

Jackson Bates of Harvard's English Department has written, "The University is a collection of mutually repellent particles held together by a common interest in parking."

A Dominican Republic blessing reads, "May those who have hunger be filled with good food and those who have an abundance of good food be filled with a hunger for justice."

"If God had wanted me to see the sunrise, she would have scheduled it later in the day!"

Leo Tolstoy: "I sit on a man's back, choking him and making him carry me, and yet assure myself and others that I am very sorry for him and wish to ease his lot by any means possible, except by getting off his neck."

"The church is a whore, but she is my mother." Shocking? Perhaps, but it portrays someone inside the church who feels the need for changes to take place, yet is a part of the very problems that are there.

A man came to my office some years ago most upset by some of the programs sponsored by the Chaplain's Office. His final parting words, as he pointed to a sign over my door, were: "You see, you even brag about it— the den of iniquity!" The sign over the door read: "The Din of Inequity."

E.E. Cummings: "Yes, celebrate everything that is not grim, dull, motionless, unrisking, inward turning. Celebrate everything that gets into the circle, that throws its heart into the tension, surprise, fear and delight of the circus, the round world, the full existence, celebrate the circus!"

"The one who dies with the most toys wins."

"War is not healthy for children and other living things."

"Blessed are the peacemakers and tranquil places little changed by time."

"Are you now, or have you ever been, AWARE?"

"When in danger, run in circles; when in doubt, scream; when cornered, smile!"

"When you believe in people, the word gets around."

I made a large poster entitled, "More four-letter dirty words" and mounted it on the wall outside my office. One of the custodians removed it, disapproving of four-letter dirty words. I hope that your ears are not too tender to hear them: Dago, trap, slum, hurt, gook, rape, dyke, hate, wasp, spic, sick, tank, pain, pimp, bomb, kike. I do believe that these four-letter words are some of the most offensive that we have.

A traditional Jewish prayer says: "Spread over us your canopy of peace."

From Exodus: "Do not follow the majority when they do wrong or when they give a testimony that perverts justice."

A Gaelic blessing:

Deep peace of the running wave to you
Deep peace of the flowing air to you
Deep peace of the quiet earth to you
Deep peace of the shining stars to you
Deep peace of the gentle night to you
Moon and stars pour out their healing light to you
Deep peace of Christ, the light of the world to you
Deep peace of Christ to you.

Abraham Heschel: "In a free society, some are guilty; all are responsible."

Pax Christi is a Catholic peace organization. They say, "The works of mercy—feed the hungry, clothe the naked, give drink to the thirsty, visit the imprisoned, care for the sick, bury the dead. The works of war—destroy crops and land, seize food supplies, destroy homes, scatter families, contaminate water, imprison dissenters, inflict wounds and burns, kill the living."

There are two lasting gifts we give our children: One is roots, the other is wings.

Robert Frost: "Home is the place where, when you have to go there, they have to take you in."

"Education is moving from cocksure ignorance to thoughtful uncertainty."

From the Sanskrit: "Look to this day, for it is life, the very life of life. In its brief course lie all the verities and realities of your existence—the bliss of growth, the glory of action, the splendor of duty. For yesterday is already a dream and tomorrow is only a vision. But today well-lived makes every yesterday a dream of happiness and every tomorrow a vision of hope. Look well, therefore, to this day, such is the salutation of the dawn."

From Greece: In war, truth is the first casualty."

Confucius: "To see the right and not to do it is cowardice."

"Here lies the tragedy of our race: not that people are poor; all people know something of poverty. Not that all people are wicked; who can claim to be good? Not that people are ignorant; who can boast to be wise? But that people are strangers."

"The Sun: The world's only inexhaustible, predictable, egalitarian, non-polluting, safe, terror-resistant and free energy source."

"The current economic system affirms the legitimacy of one-third of the world being cared for, one-third neglected, and one-third left to die or to be eliminated in small wars."

"We are not simply going to rearrange the deck chairs on the Titanic."

"War is costly, peace is priceless."

"One nuclear bomb can ruin your whole day."

"We cannot change unless we survive. We cannot survive unless we change."

"Help cure America's military-industrial complex."

"The best age is the age that you are."

"Do we fear our enemies more than we love our children?"

"Don't look back in anger nor forward in fear, but around in awareness."

Praise God with poetry and lyrical song
Praise God with the skill of the artisan
Praise God with copper and brass and bronze
Praise God with iron and steel and wax
Praise God with clay and with stylus and brush
Praise God with acrylics and pastels and chalk
Let everything that breathes praise our Lord God.

And finally, a Sioux Indian prayer:

"O great spirit, whose voice I hear in the winds, and whose breath gives life to all the world, hear me. I am small and weak. I need your strength and wisdom. Let me walk in beauty and make my eyes ever behold the red and purple sunset.

"Make my hands respect the things you have made and my ears sharp to hear your voice. Make me wise so that I may understand the things you have taught my people. Let me learn the lessons you have hidden in every leaf and rock.

"I seek strength, not to be greater than my brother, but to fight the greatest enemy, myself. Make me always ready to come to you with clean hands and straight eyes. So, when life fades, as the fading sunset, my spirit may come to you without shame."

Hebrews 12:1-2: "As for us, we have this large crowd of witnesses around us. So, then, let us rid ourselves of everything that gets in the way and of the sin which holds us so tightly, and let us run with determination the race that lies before us."

Samuel 3:11: "Speak, Lord, for your servant is listening."

Afterword

James Leslie: A short biography

Jim Leslie was born in Boston in 1925. His father, Dr. Elmer Archibald Leslie, was professor of Hebrew and Old Testament at Boston University School of Theology for 36 years; and his mother, Helen Noon Leslie, was a member of the first graduating class of Simmons College in Boston. She served as secretary to the Dean of the Agricultural School at the University of Illinois, and then became the secretary of the Rev. James Baker. Elmer and Helen met when Elmer came to serve at the church at the University of Illinois.

In 1939, at the age of 14, Jim joined his parents on a two-year world-tour sabbatical. They sailed from California to Hawaii and then on to Japan, where they stayed for several months with Elmer Leslie's former students. They visited Ohio Wesleyan missionaries Bliss and Mildred Wiant in Beijing, China. After a brief stop in Hong Kong, they traveled to India to meet with Elmer's former students who were serving as missionaries. While in India, Jim and his parents spent a day alone with Mahatma Gandhi in his mud house. They also visited with poet and Nobel laureate Tagore, who revolutionized Bengali literature.

From India, they traveled to Baghdad, Iraq; Syria; Palestine; and Lebanon. While his father visited the American University near Beirut, Jim enrolled in the American School to study French. As the Leslie family sailed from Beirut, they encountered German

U-boats in the Mediterranean Sea, so they traveled instead to Geneva, Switzerland, and then down into German-occupied France. It was with some difficulty and significant personal drama that the Leslie family eventually was able to sail back safely to New York City, where Jim's brothers and sister met them with great relief.

Jim went on to graduate from Boston University School of Theology in 1949. In 1951, he married Betty, and in June 1951, he set off for a Rotary Fellowship in England. From 1952 to 1955, Jim worked at Medford Hillside Methodist Church near Tufts University, and in 1955, he served at Harvard Epworth Methodist Church, where his father had founded Wesley Fellowship.

Also in 1955, Jim received his Ph.D. from Boston University School of Theology. Because of alphabetical assignment at the ceremony, he sat next to a comparably quiet and unassuming member of his class, Martin Luther King Jr. The two had been casual friends throughout the pursuit of their degrees.

In 1957, Jim served at Dickinson College on a Danforth grant, and in 1960, he became Ohio Wesleyan's first full-time Chaplain and Director of Religious Life; he remained in that position until 1988.

Jim and Betty had six children: Deborah; Dianne; Peter; who died at 18 months when the Leslies were at Dickenson University; Jennifer; Kristen; and Andrew.

Following his retirement from OWU, Jim and Betty continued to serve in United Methodist Volunteer in Missions work camps in Florida, Mississippi, South Carolina, Kentucky, North Carolina, New York, Texas, Louisiana, and Slovakia. Jim continues to serve in the choir at Asbury United Methodist Church in Delaware, Ohio, and as a member of the city's Martin Luther King Jr. Celebration and Scholarship Committee.

The James Leslie Center
for Peace and Justice

On October 26, 2007, at a Homecoming Gala in honor of Chaplain James Leslie, Ohio Wesleyan University announced the establishment of the James Leslie Center for Peace and Justice.

At that announcement, Chaplain Jon Powers said that the center was established "not only to honor the profound witness to peace and justice that Jim Leslie has provided to Ohio Wesleyan University since 1960, but also to ensure that Jim Leslie's commitment to peace and justice will live on in perpetuity as an integral core value of Ohio Wesleyan University in its policies and practices, its program, its partnerships, and its personal support of students, faculty, and staff at every operational level of its institutional being—globally, nationally, regionally, locally, and personally."

"We anticipate that over the years this commitment may take variant forms. However, the kinds of current commitments we immediately incorporate into the James Leslie Center for Peace and Justice provide distinct clarity for the vision we hold for this center. These programs, partnerships, and policy practices will include, but will not be limited to:

- Chaplaincy Registration of Students as Conscientious Objectors to War
- Leadership Across Boundaries, Ohio Wesleyan's newest international leadership initiative
- Partnerships with
  - Spring Break Mission Program
  - Catholic Campus Ministries

- o Amnesty International
- o OWU Buckeye Valley Reads
- o OWU Columbus Initiative
- o Crossroads Africa
- o OWU Voices for Victims of Agent Orange
- o OWU Peace and Justice House
- o OWU STAND—Student Voices for Darfur
- o CROP Walk
- o The Heifer Project
- o UNICEF
- o OWU Latino Outreach
- o Delaware's Global Village
- o Delaware's People in Need
- o Common Ground—Delaware Free Store
- o OWU Habitat for Humanity
- o Appalachia Service Project
- o John Perkins Institute for Racial Reconciliation
- o Tree of Life Ministry—Lakota Nation United Methodist Ministries
- o Sisters of Erie Benedictine Convent
- o OWU Student Initiative for International Development microfinance project
- o OWU/Ghana Student Scholarship Initiative
- o OWU National Capital Seminar: Crossroads of the Powerful and the Powerless

"It is our hope that the creation of this center for peace and justice in Jim's name will signify to Jim and his family that his presence among has permeated the woodwork of our souls. We are profoundly different people because of Jim Leslie. His life, his witness, and his work have made a difference.

"Jim we all want you to know just how much we honor you, we love you, we thank God for you, and now, through this center for peace and justice named for you, your work and your witness will live on in perpetuity. Thanks be to God."

Program Emphases of the James Leslie Center for Peace and Justice

Located within the Office of the Chaplain at Ohio Wesleyan University, the Jim Leslie Center for Peace and Justice will focus on areas of importance to its namesake. Specifically, the center will be involved with the transformational Mission Team Program, the Leadership Across Boundaries initiative, and student projects such as the Channeling Peace Initiative, all consistent with the themes of peace and justice so eloquently articulated by Jim's mentors, Mahatma Gandhi and Martin Luther King Jr.

Each year the Mission Team Program involves about 150 students, faculty, and staff in ten domestic and international mission teams. Such work is reflective of Jim's early efforts to establish these programs, including Crossroads Africa and the Haiti mission teams. The Leslie Center is built on the four foundational pillars of the Mission Team Program: Conscientious Leadership, Restorative Justice, Transformative Reflection, and Substantive Community.

Made in the USA
Charleston, SC
17 January 2011